LAST DRAW!

"Styles—" Sansome's voice was hoarse with laughter. "Styles, you ever see a man after he's been left to die with both his elbows and both his knees busted by bullets? No . . . you save 'em, don't you? Other way around with me. I've shot 'em and left 'em—"

Halting, he started to pull a careful bead on Doc's sound arm. But that one was already in motion, with a speed that no rifleman could match. Doc's hand plunged into his coat and came out with the Navy Colt. In the instant it hung level, he fired. . . .

Other *Leisure* books by T. V. Olsen:
EYE OF THE WOLF
KENO
STARBUCK'S BRAND
MISSION TO THE WEST
BONNER'S STALLION
BREAK THE YOUNG LAND
THE STALKING MOON
BLOOD OF THE BREED
LAZLO'S STRIKE
WESTWARD THEY RODE
ARROW IN THE SUN
RED IS THE RIVER
THERE WAS A SEASON

LONESOME GUN

GUN

T. V. OLSEN

LEISURE BOOKS NEW YORK CITY

A LEISURE BOOK®

August 1998

Published by special arrangement with Golden
West Literary Agency.

Dorchester Publishing Co., Inc.
276 Fifth Avenue
New York, NY 10001

ISBN 0-8439-4422-6

CHAPTER ONE

IT WAS CLOSE TO SUNSET WHEN DR. JOHN FLETCHER STYLES made camp on a western flank of the forested foothills that hedged a soaring arm of the Sweetwater Mountains. He'd been following a well-traveled wagon road that switch-backed along the slopes, and now he offsaddled in a clearing close to the road and set up his camp.

Doc Styles knew that his destination, the town of Rincon, was a little north of here. But he wasn't sure just how far, and he was dead tired. As he went about unloading his gear, hobbling his bay gelding, gathering wood, and building a fire, he was aware once more, in his grinding weariness, of what sorry shape he was in.

He was completely cured now of the consumption that had brought him to the dry Arizona climate many years ago. For his first couple of years in the West he'd led a hardy outdoor life. But his way of living after that hadn't lent itself to a robust state of health. When he hadn't been engaged in getting a deadly reputation with a gun, he'd spent half the hours of his days and nights hunched over poker tables in smoke-filled saloons and gambling halls.

A more recent and sedentary career of practicing medi-cine in the whistle-toot town of Taskerville hadn't much improved his condition. As the only physician in the place, he kept long, erratic hours. If an out-of-town patient had

1

need of his services, Doc would rent a livery team and buggy and drive out to do what he could. That was his sole exercise, and meantime the smoking and drinking habits he'd cultivated to an extent he'd flatly discourage in any of his patients had never slackened up a lot.

Setting up camp now helped limber up Doc's flaccid muscles after a second tedious day in the saddle. He dug a flask of brandy out of a saddlebag and took a long pull, then cooked up his bacon and beans and pan bread over a low fire and ravenously wolfed them down.

Afterward he stretched out on the ground, legs crossed and head pillowed on his saddle. He reached for the flask again, scowled at it, and set it aside, settling for a cigar instead. He took a "short six" from his coat pocket and wiped a match alight and held it to the cigar, still scowling as he drew in the raw and raking fumes. You couldn't afford a decent cigar on a small-town sawbones's cash income, not when most of your patients paid for your services with garden truck, eggs or milk, maybe a slab of bacon, or even on occasion a live chicken that you had to kill and dress yourself.

Damn nuisance. Hell of a comedown for a son of the Tidewater, Virginia, gentry. But Doc knew, with his usual ruthless and unsparing self-honesty, that he'd broken his own trail all the way.

Unthinkingly now, he moved a hand to his other coat pocket and pulled out Caroline's letter. He took from the envelope two sheets of paper, folded and refolded from so many rereadings that they were grimy and frayed along the creases, although he'd received the letter only three days ago. It was undated but had been posted from Rincon, only fifty miles north of Taskerville, where he'd set up his medical practice.

Carefully Doc unfolded the pages, squinted at them, and swore mildly. He took from his shirt pocket a leather case that contained a pair of wire-rimmed spectacles and grimaced as he set them on the bridge of his nose and hooked them over his ears. He needed them for any kind of close work and for reading.

It had galled the hell out of Dr. John Fletcher Styles to admit, finally, that objects close up had begun to blur in his vision. That the only remedy was the one that he'd recommended to not a few of his patients: you went to a general merchandise store and asked to see the glasses they had in stock. They set out a big case or drawerful of specs, and you tried on different ones till you came to a pair that brought things more or less into focus and rode easily on your nose and ears.

Doc couldn't even determine after a complete examination of himself, both ocular and all over, whether the condition would improve or worsen or remain about the same. What really galled the hell out of him, of course, was the old story of a man's pride—hating to admit to any debility. And God knew he had his share of pride. More than was good for any man, even after a way of life that should have ground all his stupid goddam pride into dust.

He tilted the first page of Caroline's letter against the sunset light and began to read: "My dear Fletch: I should fancy that you are more than a little surprised to hear from me after these many—"

A burst of gunfire exploded the peace of the dying day. Rifle shots, rapid-fired by a Henry or a Winchester, was his guess. And Doc Styles's ear, honed by long experience, picked out their source at once. The shooting was coming from a deep saddle between two hills, the one on whose flank he was camped, and its neighbor.

Doc sat exactly as he was for the moment, straining his ears. Nobody was shooting at him, not from several hundred yards away or through the press of tall pines that circled his camp.

Another rifle chimed in abruptly, as if returning fire.

Then, as suddenly as it had started up, all the shooting ceased.

The silence itself was a shock, for it left the forest hush deeper than before. Not a trill of birdsong. Not a murmur of squirrel chatter.

Snuffing out his cigar and then tucking his glasses and the letter away, Doc pulled his Winchester from its saddle sheath and eased to his feet. That kind of shooting wasn't from a hunter's gun. It was the kind that meant business.

He slipped into the trees and started working upward between them at a zigzag angle that would bring him out above where the sound of the shooting had come from. He went as slowly and alertly as a stalking cat. This was an old game, and Doc knew the ground rules as well as any man alive. Or he wouldn't be alive.

The afternoon heat had baked a heavy resinous smell out of the pines. It hung about him like a pungent mist. The slanting sunrays turned the clumps of pine needles to a blaze of gold burrs. A familiar tingling lay along his nerves. He'd been a long time away from the game, and there was no denying he felt a touch of the old excitement. High on the hill, close to its crown, Doc swerved right around the pine-mantled curve of its north flank to get above the point from which gunfire had come. He worked downward from there with a heightened caution. Watching. Listening.

Ahead was a break in the trees. He came to its edge and then, not wanting to get into the open, skirted it slowly, keeping a skirmish line of small pine between him and the clearing.

Doc froze at the crack of a twig. It came from downslope. Somebody was coming up toward him, trying for the same silent care of movement, but not quite successfully. His feet broke a couple more fallen twigs before he stumbled into sight across the clearing.

The man's chest was laboring. He was clutching a rifle.

And he was wounded. Blood shone on his neck and darkened the whole side of his shirt. Now he dropped to his hands and knees, shaking his head. Almost at once, though, he was back on his feet, coming up the slope again.

Holding his rifle out away from his body, one-handed, to show his good intentions, Doc stepped out of the trees. "Hold up, fella. What—"

The man didn't even hesitate.

His head swung, his wild eyes pounced on Doc, and his bearded jaws parted in a single raging shout: "Ye damn dirty *scut*—murdering son of a bitch!"

And he brought the rifle to his shoulder.

Doc yelled, "Wait, you damned fool! I just—"

But even as he spoke, even before the shot came, he was melting to the ground. The man levered his rifle and fired again. His aim was wobbly, but the shot was close enough to kick a scatter of pine-needle detritus against Doc's leg.

And then Doc had no choice. He was flat on his belly, facing the man, his arms flung out ahead of him along the ground, both hands now gripping the Winchester. Even as the man was levering his rifle to draw a third bead on him, Doc thumbed back the Winchester's hammer, tipped a quick aim, and pulled the trigger.

The bearded man was slammed over backward as if by the blow of a giant fist.

Doc levered another shell into the chamber and lay exactly as he was, only turning his head to scan the trees to the left and right and ahead of him. He was ready for anything.

Nothing. Not a whisper of sound.

Climbing to his feet, Doc tramped over to the man and dropped onto one knee beside him. A good shot. The killing kind a man pulled off when he had no time for the niceties of wing shooting. It hadn't gone quite through the heart, but it must have cut one of the big trunk arteries close to the aorta. The man's eyes rolled toward Doc, inspecting him through a blue glaze.

"Why?" Doc said, then repeated the word with a savage force: "*Why?*"

The man didn't reply. He bared his teeth in a grimace of unrelenting hate. Then his head rolled sideways. The sinking sun glinted on his short reddish beard. His eyes remained open, a rich frozen blue, and his mouth hung open.

"Goddam it all," Doc said in a soft, shaken voice. "Goddam it all to hell."

CHAPTER TWO

Moving with still-greater care, Doc went down the hillside through the clots of pine till the trees opened up once more. At the bottom of the saddle between the two hills, he found the bodies of three men.

They'd been on a wood-fetching detail; that was obvious. Many smaller pines had been cut and the logs bucked into ten-foot lengths with two-man crosscut saws. The tang of sawed wood, fresh and aromatic, hung in the stillness. Funny, Doc thought obscurely, how the aftermath of human violence left so little smell: a sulphurous whiff of powder smoke and of sphincters released in sudden death. But the odor of fresh-cut pine easily overpowered these.

Two of the men were dead. One had been hit twice, once in the lower maxilla, half tearing his jaw away, and once in the throat, a great gouting wound that had severed the carotid artery. The other's parietal bone had been bored through on the right side, and the bullet, angling downward through the brain, had emerged from the temporal bone on the left side, lifting out a large piece of his skull. Both men were bearded, roughly dressed, somewhere in their thirties.

The third man was still alive, sprawled on his face. Doc rolled him onto his back. He was out cold, but his heartbeat was strong, and all Doc could locate in the way of injury was a deep groove that ran almost down the exact center of his scalp. The bullet had bared a whitish-red streak of bone, which may have angled the slug somewhat away. Not much bleeding.

This one was considerably younger than the others. Not over eighteen and almost a mirror image, except for being beardless, of the man Doc had shot. The latter had appeared to be in his late thirties. So this one, probably, was his son or a much younger brother.

Doc coldly weighed the situation, his old instincts aroused and combative now. Whoever had ambushed the four woodcutters—Doc was sure that first volley had been fired by just one rifle—had cleared out by now. He'd downed three of his prey, wounded the fourth, and had coolly retreated when the reddish-bearded man had returned fire. Had the woodcutters expected trouble? All were equipped with rifles as well as axes and saws. But only the red-bearded man had had time to bring his weapon into play.

Slightly wounded, he'd plunged upslope toward what he'd fancied was the unseen gunner's position. And coming suddenly on Doc, he had mistaken him for the assassin.

Doc said again, distinctly, "Goddam it to hell," and swept his gaze across the dark wall of pines above the camp. At once he spotted an opening above a thrust of granite that would be an ideal vantage for a marksman.

Keeping to cover, Doc cat-footed upward and skirted around and then into the opening. On the pine-needled ground behind the outthrust, he found a litter of ejected cartridge cases. Even by full daylight, trying to follow the killer's trail across the springy carpet of needles that laced this whole hillside would be useless. All the same, Doc was cautious enough to work outward in concentric circles, looking for any chance sign. He found two dead but freshly broken twigs, each of them protruding from the boles of huge pines. Now he relaxed vigilance. The assassin had made tracks on a straight line south, and fast.

After picking up one of the cartridge cases and stowing it in his pocket, Doc tramped back down to the dead and wounded men.

On his way, he paused by the man he'd shot and searched his pockets for any identification. He found only the usual trifles a working man kept on his person. A jackknife, a leather awl, a waterproof case of matches, a plug of Star tobacco—he was a chawer, not a smoker—and a few other masculine odds and ends, none of them particularly identifying. A stocky and robust man, and a poor one. His worn clothing was much patched, although neatly and painstakingly, as if by a woman's hand. A married man, almost surely, and an Irishman. The accent had lilted strongly in his raging shout, and *scut* was a bit of purely Irish opprobrium.

What did any of it tell Doc about the real man, about the life he had wiped away? Not a goddam thing, he thought bleakly.

Doc also searched the others for identification, again finding nothing, and then prepared to pack the wounded youth out of there. He removed his own pants belt and, to improvise a rifle sling, ran the belt through his Winchester's lever and looped it around his neck so the weapon would hang down his back.

As he did so, he noticed something that hadn't struck him before. These men had been out gathering wood, all right, cutting the felled trees into uniform lengths and stacking the cut pieces in neat piles off to the side. But they'd been doing more. Looking eastward now, he saw that the tree-clearing had opened a wide avenue that followed the foothills upward. They had been laying open the right-of-way for a road that would lead out of the eastern peaks, no doubt to connect with the older wagon trace Doc had been following to Rincon. And they had nearly reached their goal.

Not bothering just now to speculate on the implications of this, Doc bent down and with a long, straining grunt lifted the unconscious youth and maneuvered him across his shoulders. Like his dead relative, the kid was only of average size, but on the chunky side—an inert dangling weight that made Doc stagger as he straightened up. But with the fireman's carry, balancing the victim across his slightly bent shoulders, one arm loosely gripping one of the kid's, the other hooked around one of his legs, even a man out of condition could pack a heavy weight quite a ways.

All the same, he was drenched with sweat, legs quivering and back aching, when he set the unconscious youth down close to the dying camp fire. By now the swift mountain twilight was overtaking the rose and gold strata of sunset beyond the westward hills. Doc rested a moment, picked up his flask and took a deep pull, then fed some dead branches into the fire to build it up.

By the aid of the flickering light, after washing the boy's scalp wound clean, he examined it more carefully, verifying his earlier judgment. He scrubbed a hand wearily over his whisker-stubbled face. The kid had a probable concussion. Nothing to do now but wait and see. There'd been little bleeding, and Doc preferred to let a wound this shallow stand open and clean to hasten the healing. The high country night that was closing down was too cold to invite insect pests. A lot of people he knew, including other medical men, would apply all kinds of things from flour to cobweb to urine—human—to such a wound—or any other—in order to cake the bleeding. In his own experience, all such treatments had proved more harmful than healing.

Doc spread one of his own blankets over the kid, then sat down tailor-fashion by the fire, got out his glasses, and clamped his cold cigar between his teeth. He took Caroline's letter once more from his pocket, shook out the pages, and spread them out on his knee, tilting them toward the fire shine:

My dear Fletch:
  I should fancy that you are more than a little surprised to hear from me after these many years. A great deal of water

and—alas!—experiences of life as well have gone under the bridge since we last communicated with each other.

Perhaps it is impertinent, if not indecent or at least selfish of me, to write you after so long. But I do not know of anyone else to whom I might turn in our present circumstances. From my last letter, sent you so long ago and which I know you must have received, although you never replied to it (quite understandably, I admit), you were aware that Alex and I were wed within two years after your departure to Arizona Territory.

As I explained that matter very thoroughly, although perhaps not at all satisfactorily, in that letter, I shan't again go into all the reasons or details thereof.

Suffice it to say that even we in the effete East were well apprised of your activities in the years following. The more unrestrained of our Virginia tabloids saw to that, as well as several yellow-backed thrillers in the tradition of Mr. Buntline's more lurid works concerning Mr. Hickok, Mr. Cody, Deadwood Dick, et cetera, that recounted (I am sure falsely or with great exaggeration) many of your own exploits.

Only recently did we learn that for some time you have been occupied with the practice of medicine in the town of Taskerville, scarcely fifty miles to the south of Rincon, where Alex and I are presently living.

As much as we may have wished to enjoy your acquaintance—and we might hope, our old friendship—once more, we did not feel justified in imposing on your present way of life, which we, perhaps wrongly, have felt is a retreat from the violence and sensationalism that had characterized your previous years in Arizona. On that speculation, of course, I can't speak with any certainty. I can only say that neither Alex nor I felt it would be wise or politic to intrude on your present mode of existence. We might only revive a host of unwelcome memories.

Now, however, this feeling is overridden by another

consideration. I tell you frankly: we are in desperate need of help and can think of nobody but you who might supply such assistance as we require.

The whole situation has become one so involved that I cannot go into it with any assurance that you may fully understand all of what it has meant, or may portend, for us and for a great many others. I have no misapprehension of your own fine intelligence, only an awareness of my personal inability to convey all of what lies at stake for so very many people.

Only Alex can fully explain the matter to you. You are a man who was always demanding of logical explanation, as he is, and only one man of logic can convey all of what he wishes to say to another.

Alex and I would have come to Taskerville to enlist your aid in person but for the fact that Alex's physical condition is such that any protracted journey, at present, is out of the question.

Fletch, I know that this pathetic epistle, coming from one old friend to another, must have a quality that is strained and stiff. It is written under great stress. It is the appeal of one who is making an awkward (and confessedly selfish) attempt to use a former relationship to further an end which is of utmost importance to her.

I shall not blame you if you ignore this letter or simply consign it to a wastebasket. Yet, for the sake of the feeling that once existed so strongly among the three of us, you and Alex and I, I beg you to have forbearance toward this imposition on a friendship that was.

For the next two weeks, I shall come every day to the Fuller House in Rincon (its only respectable hostelry) in hopes that you have registered there. If you do so, please sign your name as J. Fletcher.

> Yours as warmly as ever,
> Caro
> (Mrs. Alexander Drayton)

Doc pulled a burning twig from the fire's edge and lighted up his cigar.

Very good. A well-written letter. Not that he'd expect less of her. The former Caroline Varina Carter had always been clever with words, as he remembered from letters she'd sent him at the front during the war. He could visualize her, as he'd done often enough—but always as he'd last seen her, God, nearly two decades ago—seated at a cheap and scarred desk or table writing on this cheap notepaper—quite a contrast to the thick, elegant yellow-cream stationery she'd once used—composing and discarding several versions of this letter in order to get an exact effect with each phrase, each word.

Doc yawned and leafed through the pages again, squinting against the swirl of cigar smoke.

It was a genuine plea for help; the desperate note it carried was real. Also, she was as fervently an idealist as was Alex Drayton, the man she had wed. And as John Fletcher Styles had been in the bygone time when he and Caroline had become engaged, ending—temporarily—the rivalry over her between him and Drayton, who had been one of his closest friends. There were touches of ambiguity, as well, mainly the request that he register at the hotel under his first initial and middle name, suggesting she didn't want it bruited about—at least not right away—that the notorious Doc Styles was in the neighborhood.

Very neat, also, were the small, careful turns of phrase calculated to hit every nerve of his nature. Touches of flattery for his male arrogance. Little interjections of modest apology for imposing on his new life. Reminders of the closeness that had been among Alex and her and him. An appeal to the idealism they all had shared—"what lies at stake for so many people." And the very warm closing that reminded him that she was Mrs. Alexander Drayton—or, Don't get any ideas, boy. Underneath it all ran a shrewd current of knowledge that he was still, probably, an incurable goddam sentimentalist who couldn't resist the appeal of a vanished past, a lost love. Just as shrewd was her gamble that if, by not divulging the reason behind her request, she could pique his curiosity enough to fetch him to Rincon—as she had—half her battle might be won.

In an abrupt burst of anger, he almost balled the letter in his fist and flung it into the fire. Then he smoothed the half-crumpled sheets and restored them to the envelope and his pocket. He stretched his legs and drew deeply on the cigar, musing wearily.

There was a low groan from the wounded youth. Doc rose and stepped around the fire to lay a hand on the kid's forehead. Fever. A sluggish stir of eyelashes, too. Yet the kid didn't open his eyes.

Good boy, thought Doc. You ought to be fine as snuff before long. I just hope when you are, you don't get making the same mistake that relative of yours did.

CHAPTER THREE

Next morning, about an hour after breaking camp, Doc rode the off-tapering swell of the foothills into a slot of valley that held the town of Rincon.

It was a god-awful bedlam of racket to ride into after two days and nights on a meandering trail that passed over lonely forested hills and through tranquil silences broken only by the hush of wind and the chatter of small birds and animals.

Rincon was a roaring hellbroth of a town that violated all his senses even before he reached its outskirts. The main street was jammed with ore wagons on their way to or from the irregular scatter of mines on the northern slopes above. Saddle horses and rigs of all kinds, carriages and buckboards, crowded the hitchracks of the single street's five or six blocks. Teamsters were yelling and cursing and cracking whips above the mules' heads.

From the saloons and gambling dives came an unintelligible din of noise. A lot of it was from the throats of miners of many nationalities, gabbling away in their native tongues. They flowed in and out of the gambling halls and saloons, talking loudly, swearing with abandon, earning curses from the teamsters as they threaded across the mud-rutted streets in front of or between the wagons. Even the worst of the western boomtowns Doc had seen would have to come up—or down—a few notches to equal this display of raw turmoil.

At each end of town the business places consisted of big canvas tents with crudely lettered signs stuck in the ground out front. The farther he rode into the heart of Rincon, the more substantial the buildings became. As this was a well-timbered country, there were plenty of frame buildings as well as cabins and even, toward the center of town, a couple of two-story brick structures. On a couple of streets that branched off the main one, Doc noted several buildings with gaudy signs proclaiming them to be boardinghouses—namely, whorehouses. Damned near as many, probably, as there were saloons, even if they tended to be demurely tucked off on side streets. Sandwiched together, the watering places and cathouses would account for about half the business activity in a town like Rincon.

Doc was feeling edgy and half deafened as he swung stiffly off his mount in front of a tall frame building that had a crude stairway running up one outside wall. It led to a second-story doorway with the legend *H. R. Kroll, M.D.* lettered above it.

A few people on the boardwalks halted to stare, adding to Doc's irritability as he tied up his gelding and walked around behind it to bend over the Indian-style horse drag he'd rigged up to carry the injured youth. The kid was still semiconscious and running a high fever. Afterward Doc tramped up the stairway to H. R. Kroll's doorway. He knocked at it off and on for a full minute before the door opened.

Kroll was a small, wizened man with sparse and rumpled white hair who smelled strongly of ether and antiseptic solutions and, more subtly, whiskey. He was in his shirt-sleeves, rubbing a wet towel over his face, and was obviously in poor humor. One of the genuine brotherhood, thought Doc.

Not revealing his own medical status, Doc gave Kroll the briefest sketch of how he'd found the kid, omitting any mention of the fact that he'd shot and killed an obvious relative of the boy's. He also offered a modest suggestion that the kid might have what he'd once heard a back-home sawbones describe as a "concussion."

Some of the bleary look washed out of Kroll's eyes. He gave a testy grunt, pitched the wadded-up towel aside, and said, "Well, let's get him up here. If you'll be so kind as to lend me a hand."

Between them, the two untied the boy from the travois and carried him up to a back room in the doctor's quarters. Doc asked Kroll, politely and casually, if he had any idea who the lad might be. Kroll allowed that he did, to a point. The kid came from one of the settler families living up on Redondo Flats way above the town and had an older brother; their last name was O'Hearn, and that's all he knew about them.

To Doc's next question, Kroll replied that the county seat was way across the mountains, eastward. That's where the sheriff's office was, and that's where county law held any real sway, if you wanted to appeal to it. The only law in this boom-or-bust mining town was a town marshal appointed by the miners' council, which was a bunch of big-ass muckamucks that ran the big mining companies. When the muckamucks said frog, their marshal jumped. He was, Kroll went on to say, a potbellied asshole named Harry Rich, and if Doc wanted to direct this matter to his attention, it wouldn't do a damn lick of good. Even if Rich had any jurisdiction outside of Rincon, which he didn't, he couldn't care less.

"What about the dead men?" Doc asked.

"No need to worry about it," Kroll told him. "When those men don't return home, their families will send to find out why not. They'll recover the bodies and do their own burying and mourning. That's how it is up on the Redondo Flats."

"I'll pay for the boy's care and keep," said Doc, pulling out his wallet. "And I'll come in to check on him."

Dr. Kroll shrugged. "If it suits you. He might be up and around by this time tomorrow."

"Do you have any idea who might have shot them, doctor?"

"You say it appeared to be the work of one man?"

Doc nodded.

"Around here, my friend, that kind of speculation could cover a lot of territory. For a lot of reasons."

Kroll's face had closed up, and Doc knew he wouldn't commit himself to any particular suspicions.

Doc thanked his colleague, went down the outside stairway, climbed into his saddle, and headed back toward the bustling midtown. Riding in, he had noted the locations of the Fuller House and the local livery barn. He left his gelding at the barn with orders for its care and feeding and told the hostler to discard the travois poles.

Afterward, carrying his war bag and saddlebags, his rifle and canteen, Doc entered the lobby of the nearby Fuller House, a weathered firetrap of a building. He asked for a room, put on his glasses to sign in as *J. Fletcher*, paid up for a night's stay, received his key, and went up to the second-story room. It contained a bed with grayish worn but clean sheets and a battered washstand. Doc deposited his belongings on the floor and then, realizing he was hungry, stepped out, locked his door, and left the hotel.

Outside on the porch, he paused long enough to take out a short six and light it up, glancing along the street and noting that the Red Star Cafe was located diagonally across from the hotel. He stepped off the porch and started across to the café, over a mire of maroon mud that had been chopped into craters and canyons by boots and hooves and wagon-wheel ruts. Picking his way with care through a casual rumble of traffic that had thinned out a little since earlier, Doc tried to stick to solid-looking patches of ground.

He was nearly to the other side when he was surprised to a stop. The wild yellings, punctuated by a popping of gunshots, reached him before he caught a first glimpse of the riders.

They came veering out of one of the side streets, ten or twelve of them, firing their sidearms at the sky and hollering their heads off. Cutting around the block just a few yards ahead of where Doc stood, they came bearing down on him, straight and sudden.

Doc made a wild dive sideways to get out of their path. He fell face-down in the mud. For a moment he was blinded by dirty water, by his own panic, and by the group of riders thundering by just a few feet away.

Doc dragged himself to his knees and then to his feet, grabbing for support at the tie rail in front of the Red Star Cafe. Blinking his eyes clear, he realized that his glasses, which he'd neglected to remove after signing the hotel register, were left somewhere in the mud.

Bending down to find them, he heard one of the riders yell, "Hey there! Sorry about tha', Four-Eyes!"

They had pulled up in front of the Shortbough Saloon next to the Fuller House—all of them except the young olive-skinned fellow who had laughed and yelled. He was still sitting his horse, and now, even as the other riders were leathering their six-guns and piling off their mounts, the youth raised his gun again and fired.

Doc felt a savage flare of pain in his face. A long splinter torn from the tie rail where he was leaning had ripped into his cheek. He jerked away from the tie rail, grabbing at the left side of his face to pull the splinter free.

The youth fired again, this shot tearing more shards from the tie rail. None of them hit Doc, but he flinched backward, and his bootheel hooked on the boardwalk. He crashed on his back across the muddied boards, his head rapping hard against the Red Star Cafe steps.

The whole crowd of horsemen, as they dismounted, burst into laughter. It had a sound that was good-natured but also raw and raucous. They were all as drunk as skunks. In the few moments that Doc lay sprawled and helpless, they had a long, loud laugh at his expense.

The young olive-skinned fellow, on his feet beside his

horse now and grinning, raised his pistol and pointed it in Doc's direction once more.

He fired two more shots, chewing up wood from the steps about a foot to either side of Doc's head. The gun roar was deafening. Doc lay dead still, just watching this crazy shootist. A shit-brained lunatic like him might try anything next. You never knew.

"Hey, Señor Four-Eyes. How you like it if—!"

"Quit it, Gregorio. No more of that, you hear?"

The man who spoke, the apparent leader of this bunch, was looping his reins around the tie rail in front of the Shortbough Saloon, as were the other riders. All were grinning or chuckling. The leader, a tall and solidly built man with curling gray hair, was also amused, but he plainly meant what he'd said.

"Sure, Elmo, tha's all right. It's what you say, eh?"

"Just so you remember it," Elmo said gently.

Still staring at Doc, showing his upper teeth and gums in what wasn't a real grin, the olive-skinned kid holstered his gun, tied up his horse, and sauntered along with his companions into the Shortbough.

Doc hauled himself to his feet and made another sagging grasp at the tie rail. All of one side of his coat and trousers was plastered with mud. His short six was mashed across his cheek, and he wiped away its remnants with one hand. He had to squint carefully about before he located his glasses in the mud beside the porch. Fumbling out a handkerchief, he cleaned every speck of dirt off and tucked them in his pocket.

A hot killing rage filled his mind.

With his hunger forgotten, Doc slogged back across the street. He entered the hotel and tramped across the lobby toward the stairway, the caked mud crumbling away from his clothes.

Maybe he looked as murderous as he felt. As he went past the lobby desk, the gaping clerk seemed about to say something. Then he swallowed and closed his mouth.

CHAPTER FOUR

IN HIS ROOM DOC HELD A COLD, WET CLOTH TO HIS FACE TO
check the bleeding. Then he stripped off his coat and vest
and shirt. The vest was fairly clean, the white shirtfront
conspicuously spattered. He had an extra shirt in his war
bag; he could clean the worst of the mud from his trousers,
and they would do for a while. The coat, though, would
need a thorough cleaning. Meantime, the vest alone would
serve. Just about everyone in a rough high-country mining
town went about in their shirt-sleeves, weather permitting.
He wiped the mud from his boots and trousers, then got out
the fresh shirt and slipped it on over his head. He fastened
his collar in place and stood in front of the stained mirror
above the washstand to adjust his cravat.

Gazing at his reflection, Doc's fingers stilled. He wondered what Caroline would think—after so many years.

Not that he was unrecognizably different. Medium
height, slim and wiry build, easy and yet cat-quick in his
movements—God's gifts to a sinner, maybe—that's how
she'd remember him. Now he looked trim enough but
heavier set, with the added weight of just getting older. It
gave him a false look of stocky strength.

Doc's face was strong, too, in a bony, narrow-jawed way.
His ash-blond hair was cut short these days, and his fair
mustache drooped past the corners of his mouth. His eyes

were of the palest blue and even in amiable repose gave off an unblinking stare that had disconcerted more than one man who'd tried conclusions with him.

What will you think of it now, Caro? It was a sad and fleeting thought.

Turning, Doc picked up his blanket roll, carried it to the bed, and unrolled it. Inside was a shoulder-rig gun belt, oil-rubbed till it was shining and flexible except for the stiffened holster, which contained a .36 Navy Colt revolver, Model 1861, converted to take metal cartridges.

As Doc strapped it on, his mind turned back to the long-gone time when Sharp Sam Buttrick had given him the crucial advice that had likely saved his life several times. Wild and embittered, having had his whole world cave in on him just when he'd gotten back his health, Doc had been grazing against all kinds of hellfire situations in Tucson. He'd even set out to become a cross-draw artist, because the best gunman he'd met to date had been one.

"Listen, boy," Sharp Sam, who had taken a liking to him, had told him in a kindly way, "if you got to keep your pecker up with the aid of a goddam firearm in order to settle your difficulties, do it right or you won't last out a week. First off, you got a problem with your reach. Your forearm is too goddam short compared to your upper arm. Hard to reach acrost your body that way. Try it— See what I mean? What you need is—you need a goddam shoulder rig. I see you do a lot of gambling at tables. All right, if you're sitting acrost a table from somebody gets pissed off and pulls iron on you, you gonna have one helluva time getting out a gun from the hip soon enough if you're sitting four square on your ass, heh? All you need is just to reach for a shoulder gun and you got your edge."

Doc, knowing Sharp Sam to be one of the best, had listened and learned.

The shoulder harness Sam had ordered for him was the one he still owned: a flexible belt strapped around his chest with a leather extension that fastened on his left side and looped over his shoulder to a hitch on the back of the belt. Where the belt and shoulder loop met in front, the holster— stiff enough to avoid hanging-up a pistol as it was pulled free—was anchored. What he needed to fill the holster, Sharp Sam had said, was a goddam .36 Navy Colt, smaller and lighter than the Army .44 Doc had been using. The latter was a hell of a drag on a man's arm. Also, it was damned uncomfortable to wear that way, almost under the arm. And the goddam front sight should be filed so's not to snag on Doc's coat when he pulled iron.

Sharp Sam had been right on all counts. Middle-aged, too handy with a gun himself, by then drinking himself to death on account of it, he'd nevertheless passed on to Doc all his own hard-won lore in the course of a few boozy evenings. Less than a month later, Sam was killed in a drunken shoot-out in which he'd stood considerably less than an even chance.

Doc had heeded Sam's advice on becoming a shootist, but what else he might have learned from Sam's example hadn't taken. Not back then it hadn't.

Now the shoulder harness and the weight of its holstered gun had an odd, unfamiliar feel, strapped on after five years.

Doc walked back to the mirror and looked at himself again. His lip curled. Old Deadeye Doc himself, all set to plunge back into what he'd tried so long to pass off and forget. Just, for Christ's sake, because some punk brat had badgered him on a random, drunken whim. Seeing himself as he once had been made the ruthless rage in Doc dwindle. He felt it withering back to cold ashes even as a soft knock came at the door.

Unconsciously, Doc's right arm bent up. His hand was close to the walnut butt of his revolver as he moved to the door and opened it.

Caroline Drayton's eyes widened. Her first view of John

Fletcher Styles after seventeen years was seeing him in an armed, defensive posture. But she only said quietly, "Fletch . . . may I come in?"

Doc dropped his right hand and moved aside so she could step into the room. His left hand still rested on the doorknob as he gave her an inquiring glance. Caroline smiled faintly.

"You may close the door or leave it open, Fletch."

"It depends," he said dryly, "on what's preferable, Caro. Privacy or propriety?"

"Neither, with an old friend, should be of great account."

He left the door open, and they stood gazing at each other.

The clean-cut, exquisite beauty of Caroline's girlhood had lasted into her fortieth year. A fine webbing of lines at the corners of her eyes, a touch of gray in the backsweep of her dark piled hair, couldn't detract from it. She was wearing a dove-gray skirt and a short, fur-trimmed gray traveling cape. Open at the throat, it showed the snowy white of her shirtwaist, fastened at its top by a silver pin with a jade setting that matched her eyes, exactly.

Doc knew that pin. It had been a gift from him. A lifetime ago.

Seeing where his glance held, Caroline fingered the pin. "I didn't put it on just for today, Fletch," she said quietly. "I wear it quite often. You're looking remarkably well."

"Appearances can be deceiving. It would be superfluous to remark on how kindly time has treated you."

"Nevertheless"—her smile reached into him like the flick of a knife tip—"a woman likes to hear it said."

"Beautiful as ever. But married."

Caroline laughed gently. "You put it so dryly, Fletch, but you always did say things just so. Not bitterly, I mean, I don't even think cynically—"

"Just dryly. I know." Doc's tone remained easy and polite. "Alex didn't come with you?"

She shook her head, her look turning shaded and sober. "He's not well. And his condition hasn't improved since I wrote you. I thought we might confer at our house."

Doc walked to the bed, where he had laid his vest out to dry. It was a little damp but wearable. As he shrugged into it, Caroline said to his back, "Thank you for coming, Fletch. . . . I wasn't at all sure whether you would."

Doc turned, smiling faintly as he adjusted the vest loosely across his shoulder rig, thinking, *Yes you were.* Aloud he said, "I'll have to dispense with the dignity of a coat for a while. Had an accident with mine. Shall we go?"

They left the hotel and turned north along the boardwalk. A raucous din of mirth rolled out of the adjoining Shortbough. The riders who'd hoorawed him, whoever they were, must be making a day of it. Caroline tucked her hand inside the crook of his arm as they headed upstreet. In the thin coolness of this high country, the warm blaze of the midday sun was pleasant against their backs.

Raising his voice so he'd be heard above the confused racket of traffic, Doc said, "Caro, what's this all about, anyway?"

"I think Alex should tell you in his own words. You two always had such a meeting of minds. So logical, the both of you! I always envied you fellows your intellects."

Mock modesty. Caroline had an excellent mind of her own. But logic—Christ, what in this world was logical? The older you got, the less anything made sense.

Her touch, her closeness, made his thoughts tip backward with an explosive, vicious nostalgia. He'd thought he was long dead to any pain of this intensity. But there it was, lingering like a banked fire.

As the son of an affluent Tidewater family, young John Fletcher Styles had been able to get all his medical training abroad: in Berlin, Heidelberg, Vienna. Caroline and he had been secretly pledged to each other even before that, when he was sixteen and she only fourteen.

Just after his return from Europe had come the firing on
Sumter, the detonation of war. Both he and his then-closest
friend, Alexander Drayton, had promptly enlisted in Lee's
Army of Northern Virginia. They had fought side by side
through the early hopeless fight to save western Virginia,
later in the Seven Days Battle on the Chickahominy, at
Second Manassas, Antietam, Fredericksburg, Chancellors-
ville, and finally—for young Dr. Styles—at Gettysburg,
where he'd caught what was probably a stray or randomly
fired slug.

For days he had lain between life and death in one field
hospital or another till he was sufficiently recovered to be
invalided to his family home and Caroline's constant,
devoted care. By war's end he was back on his feet and
engaging in private medical practice. But he'd never made a
complete comeback. Apparently the bullet had touched a
lung. No specialist that he'd consulted could offer a sure
diagnosis. By the spring of 1866, consumption had taken
hold, and his health was failing fast.

The only recommendation from his colleagues that had
made sense at the time was that he seek the salubrious
climate of Arizona Territory. There, stimulated by a hardy
outdoors life, his health had improved. Enough so that at
the end of two years he made a decision to send for Caroline
and ask her to join him in a wide-open country where the
possibilities seemed unlimited.

A day after he sent the letter off, Caroline's own lengthy
and explanatory letter had arrived like a thunderbolt. She
and Alex Drayton had been wed. That letter, to which he'd
never replied, had changed the course of his life. Before
he'd finally extricated himself, years later, from a morass of
self-pity, drinking and gambling, picking vicious quarrels,
and joining in public feuds of one sort or another, he'd
become the renowned and deadly "Doc" Styles.

But nowadays, when men called him Doc, it was a term of easy-feeling friendship. And of trust.

Caroline gave him a fleeting, possibly inquiring glance and smile. Rousing himself from his morose silence, he pleasantly asked where she and Alex lived.

"There."

Caroline pointed a gloved hand at a slope above the west side of town, an incline that began as a mild upward grade and then soared into a tall bulwark of cliffs. He saw a rough cabin of unpeeled logs isolated on the tawny flank of the lower slope, perched in solitude. House? It seemed more of a shack.

As if she sensed his thought, Caroline said, "Alex is the local assayer, Fletch. The only one around with any real qualifications. He analyzes ore samples and such that are brought to him by single-claim miners. His office is there. It's also our home."

Doc thought that, yes, that would be like Alex. Always a quiet and studious fellow, preoccupied with subjects like arithmetic and chemistry. It hadn't prevented him from becoming Doc's main rival in the courting of Caroline, however. Or from being a wryly agreeable loser when she had remained unshakable in her betrothal to Doc.

That's what he'd never forgotten or forgiven. Alex's taking advantage of his departure for Arizona to resume an ardent wooing of the girl they both loved. Doc had refused to wed Caroline unless and until he was certain of renewed health. An absent fiancé didn't cut much of a swatch. Not for a girl now into her twenties and too aware of how fast time was passing for her.

Hell. None of it mattered anymore. Alex had won.

They left the main street of Rincon where, toward the north end, it dwindled off into a few isolated buildings. Then they trudged up the flinty slope along a badly defined road that switchbacked up to the squat cabin a few hundred feet above.

As they halted on the stoop outside and Caroline opened the door, Doc felt an increasing curiosity as to why a mining town's only assayer, especially if the town was at the peak of its boom days, as Rincon seemed to be, should be reduced to living in a log shack. You'd think there'd be such a terrific demand for his professional services from the big mining outfits that Alex and Caroline could live on a comfortable level.

They stepped into the front room.

Doc knew at once that he was standing in an assayer's office. He'd seen the like of it before in mining regions. There was a deal table that held a glass-cased set of sample balances, and laid alongside it, a sheet of paper with some mathematical calculations scrawled on it. An assay furnace stood in one corner, and there was a plank bench covered with cupels, flux bins, molds, sample sacks, and tongs. Alex Drayton was deep into the assaying business, all right.

Remembering what he did of Alex's abilities, Doc thought, He's a damned good one, I'll bet. Then how did all this poverty come about?

Caroline moved to a doorway at the back of the office. It was separated from the room behind by a broad strip of burlap. She pushed the burlap curtain aside and called softly, "Alex?"

There was a stir of movement in the back room. Alex Drayton came out. Massaging his eyelids with a thumb and forefinger, he wore the seedy, groggy look of a man suddenly awakened from sleep. Then he came to a halt, staring.

"Fletch!" Alex crossed the room in a few hobbling strides, his hand reaching out to grasp Doc's. "Lord, boy, it's good to see you again!"

Doc was a little thrown off by the warm sincerity of the greeting. But his reaction went beyond that. In a moment all the resentment he'd harbored against Alex Drayton vanished as if it had never been.

Sweet Jesus.

Alexander Drayton was Doc's age, forty-two. But he had thinned to a wraith of his old self. Never a large man, not really slight, either, he looked bent and shrunken beyond his years. His sandy hair had gone completely gray, the sparkling blue of his eyes faded to a few kindling lights. His face, once thinly handsome, was drawn and haggard, withered almost to a lined caricature of what it had been. His limping twisted-foot stride, which looked as if the right leg would hardly take his weight, was shocking to see.

Yet he was still Alex Drayton. The fresh, quick smile was the same, as was the warm friendship that glowed from his face. Like Doc, he was in his shirt-sleeves; he still wore dark broadcloth with a kind of somber elegance, but the trousers and vest were shabby from too much wear, wrinkled from being slept in.

Awkwardly now, with Caroline's help, Alex cleaned a couple of battered wooden armchairs of the ore samples that littered them and motioned Doc toward one. "Caro was sure you'd show up. I wasn't. Wouldn't have blamed you if you hadn't."

Doc shuttled a glance at Caroline. A soft flush of color touched her face. That wasn't what she'd told him. He slumped into the chair, and Alex took the other one. Caroline was already heading toward the back room, murmuring, "I'll fix some coffee," as she went past the burlap drape.

"Maybe you'd better just get to it, Alex. Caroline didn't tell me much. What is it you want of me?"

"Before I tell you, I'll have to lay out the whole situation as it stands. Can you bear with me awhile?"

"I reckon," Doc said dryly. "After coming this far, I'd better."

CHAPTER FIVE

Alex leaned forward, resting his elbows on his knees, hands clasped loosely in front of him. "Have you heard of Matthew Cordwainer?"

Doc shrugged. "Who hasn't? He's one of the big names in the Territory."

"Yes. Among other things, he owns controlling interests in quite a few mines and a couple of ore-reduction mills hereabouts. And throws a lot more weight than that. He has connections on the Pacific coast. The big bankers there will back any scheme of his to almost any amount of credit, based on speculation, because they've learned it pays off in the end. And what we have right here looks very good to Cordwainer."

"'We'?"

Alex explained that the mining companies that had set up in the lower Sweetwater range had run into trouble when their straight-down mine shafts had begun to fill with water. It had prevented them from digging any deeper for ore deposits that still lay untapped. During a casual meeting with Matthew Cordwainer in San Francisco a couple of years ago, Alex had mentioned to the mining magnate that the problem could doubtless be solved by a tunnel being driven into the base of the Sweetwater range on its western side—where Cordwainer owned plenty of property—penetrating through earth and rock until it met the main shafts of the flooded mines at a depth of roughly two thousand feet.

Alex paused. "You'll remember that I had a considerable interest in mine engineering . . . even before the war. After Caroline and I were wed, I took up those studies in earnest. Gained a fair reputation in the field, and it's proved to be highly remunerative. Caro and I have fared well over the years. Well, Matthew Cordwainer was taken by my idea of running in a tunnel that would drain the main shafts of water. Enough to offer me two dollars per ton of ore that would be taken out of the drained ground . . . if I'd personally supervise the job of putting the tunnel through."

Alex took out a pipe and pouch of tobacco and began slowly, absently, to fill the pipe bowl.

"Doesn't sound like a half-bad bargain," Doc observed in a neutral voice.

"Not at all. Quite a lucrative one from my viewpoint."

"But something went wrong. What?"

Alex bit hard on the stem of his pipe. "Way up above here, Fletch, above the town and the mines, is Redondo Flats. It's plateau country, sort of a big swatch carved out of the peaks. Rough in places but mostly level. Good grazing land here and there. Some Mexicans took up ranching there years back, after they'd been pushed out of the low country by some big Anglo ranchers. You're familiar with the pattern, I'm sure. Sometime after that, a few hardscrabble Anglo cowhands, independent cusses who wanted to get a start on their own, settled in with them, married up with some of their women. All the cattle outfits up on the Flats are one loop, you understand, very small potatoes. But it's a way of life with them . . . and the only means of survival, on any terms, for them and their families.

"Getting water to their cattle is the biggest consideration for each outfit. They have access to a few mountain streams and a scattering of springs. Cattle need a watering place inside a convenient distance. If they don't find it, they drift.

Then you have a lot of lost cows, a heavy winterkill, a hell
of a time working all the strays out of the breaks and draws.

"To make a long story short, I ran Cordwainer's tunnel
through for him and tapped one of the flooded mines. It
worked like a charm. Overnight that mine, the Lucky Lady,
was drained of water to the two-thousand-foot depth. What
else happened was that the water level in the springs and up
on the Redondo Flats began to drop fast . . . literally
overnight. I didn't hear about it right away. I laid out plans
for branches of the tunnel that would tap a half-dozen more
shafts. And then I destroyed all of them—all of the plans—
so that Cordwainer couldn't make use of them. And I quit
him cold."

"Let me guess," said Doc, trying not to sound resigned.
"You realized that tunnel of yours was drawing water from
up above. Draining off those poor folks' sources of
livelihood."

"Exactly. Destroying their whole watershed." Alex
paused to strike a match and hold it to his pipe bowl, puffing
it alight. "I was damned if I'd help Cordwainer or his
cohorts add more millions to their bloated pocketbooks at
the expense of people who hardly had anything to start with.
Fletch, have you heard of a man named Powell? Major John
Wesley Powell?"

"Some. Fellow who explored the Grand Canyon of the
Colorado and a lot more of the river. Shortly after the war,
wasn't it?"

"Yes. He did more. Powell was a U.S. government
geologist. Submitted a meticulously detailed report to
Congress on the damage that the settlers, both cattlemen
and farmers, had already done to the western lands.
Overgrazed and overcropped them until the topsoil was
stripped, a plaything for wind and rain. Worn gradually
away until it set a pattern for destruction, even wholesale
disaster. Powell also suggested a revolutionary plan for
classifying the western lands so that certain areas could be
used only for mining, others only for lumbering or grazing,

and so on. Congress ignored the report. Ever since Powell submitted his findings, they've been gathering dust in the federal archives."

Alex was flushed with his own intensity; he stabbed his pipestem at Doc. "Probably I was the first to dust off Powell's treatises and give them a thorough reading. I did it when Caro and I were living in Washington a few years back. Powell's predictions convinced me. I've seen enough to know that what he claimed would happen *is* happening. One of our most abiding sins is our profligate waste of water. Well, that's what's being done here and now, by greedy mineowners who are draining water out of the mountains, off the heights of land, for their immediate profit. A few men destroying the value of the land on which the many depend for bare survival. As long as the rich men get theirs, to hell with everyone else. And to hell with the future of America!"

Same old Alex. Get him wound up on an idealist cause and he'd unwind like a haywire clock springing its innards. Allowing that he himself had once been the same way, Doc said tolerantly, "Mmm," slowly nodding.

"My destroying the maps and quitting Cordwainer didn't change anything, of course," Alex went on. "He simply hired another mining engineer—one of the best in our field—to make out the same calculations for tapping the other Cordwainer mines. The tunneling went ahead with predictable results. The springs and streams up on Redondo Flats are slowly draining away to trickles."

Doc crossed his arms and lifted one shoulder in a mild shrug. "Yes?"

"Well, I felt partly to blame for what was bound to happen on the Flats. Right after I quit Cordwainer, I approached the Flats people and offered my help in checking the damage being wreaked on their land. I organized a group of them, and we went to Santa Fe to petition the territorial government for help. It did no good. Matthew Cordwainer swings too much weight in the capital. The official response, of course, was that he and his fellow moguls were operating within the law."

Again Alex paused, thrusting out his pipestem. "Then I came up with an answer of my own. Back in the early fifties, even before the Mexicans settled up on the plateau, an Anglo speculator named Richardson drove a mine shaft into the Flats where they backed up against the peaks. Sank quite a lot of money into the project before he abandoned it. But his diggings extended way down below a thousand feet. A full vertical mine shaft, drift tunnels branching off, and all the timbering that had been done, braces and stulls and so on, were still intact. A wildcat venture that Richardson gave up when, finally, it didn't pay off. But just out of curiosity I went down into that mine. In one of the drift tunnels I found a cross fault that looked promising. Some of it, maybe, was just a strong intuitive hunch. But I dug into the fault and personally assayed some of the ore samples.

"Fletch, there's a fortune in silver-bearing ore waiting down there for anyone who can afford to take it out. It's *above* flood level, and you'd never guess what its worth might be."

Doc smiled a little, trying to look interested. "I don't reckon. What?"

"Half a million dollars. That's a minimal estimate. It might come to well over a million. What I did next was, I persuaded the Flats people, some of whom had so far occupied their property with no legal aegis, to go to the county seat, where the U.S. Land Office is headquartered, and get their lands registered under the Homestead Act. All of them did. The homestead claims that now solidly range across that whole area should cover, if my estimations are correct, a silver-bearing vein of ore that will yield ten times anything that Cordwainer or his people have tapped to date."

Caroline came out of the back room, carrying two steaming cups of coffee. She handed a cup to each of them, then walked back to the doorway, leaned her back against the doorjamb, and folded her arms, watching them.

Doc nodded his thanks and said nothing. Alex sipped his coffee.

"The Flats people couldn't scrape together enough to get any big-scale mine operation under way. So Caro and I sank all our savings, which were considerable, into further development of the silver range. It wasn't entirely an altruistic decision. We drew up a cooperative agreement with the Flats people beforehand. My commission would be equal to what I'd have realized from Cordwainer for putting his tunnel through . . . and if I was right about this strike, we could make enough out of it to support Caroline and myself comfortably for the rest of our lives. The Redondo Flats people would benefit tremendously as well. And a lot of payroll money could be saved if the menfolk would provide the manual labor for their own mines."

Doc drank off half his coffee. "Sounds like a choice idea."

"Was and is. There was a snake in Eden. When Matthew Cordwainer found out what we were up to and was convinced we had our fingers in a big pot, he made the Flats people a reasonably good offer for all their land, all the mineral rights thereof, to become effective on the date all the homesteads were proved up. I advised them not to accept, to stand fast. All of them did—which took some courage on their part. Cordwainer was holding out sure money, after all, against my educated gamble. It was a vote of confidence in *me*. When his offers didn't take, Cordwainer imported a crew of tough nuts to harass us. They're headed by a fellow named Elmo Jagger—"

"I've heard the first name," Doc broke in gently. "Think I almost met the man."

"How's that?"

Doc told them all of it, everything that had happened since he'd gotten Caroline's letter. The only thing he omitted, as he had with Dr. Kroll, was that his bullet had downed the man named O'Hearn.

When he'd finished, both Alex and Caroline were gazing straight at him, their faces pale and shocked.

"God." Alex scrubbed a hand over his face, slowly. When he dropped the hand, his look was sick and drained. "Cordwainer is really out for blood now. Willing to go all the way, it seems. The murdered man Kroll identified for you was Thomas O'Hearn. The wounded one you brought in is his younger brother, Danny Mike. The other men who were killed—" He lifted his shoulders and let them fall. "They might have been any of the other settlers from the flats."

Doc nodded slowly. At least two of the men had looked as if they might have a heritage of Indian or Mexican blood.

"They all banded together, you see," Caroline put in quietly. "Tom O'Hearn was their leader, Fletch. He—" She lowered her eyes.

"May as well say it out, Caro." Alex smiled crookedly. "I'm not a fighting man—"

"You're not a coward, either," Caroline said quickly.

"I hope not. But I failed abysmally in trying to organize the Flats people into anything like a fighting force. The talent that Cordwainer imported, Elmo Jagger and his crew, made several forays on our mine. I suspect to dynamite it and cave in the tunnels. We anticipated such a move. Each time they tried it, we were ready. We turned back everything they threw against us. Evidently Cordwainer thought I was behind the strategy of our defense. . . ."

"And so," said Caroline, "Cordwainer had an ambush laid for Alex. Had him shot as he was riding up to the Flats."

"Whoever did the shooting," said Alex, "must have been well apprised of my routine doings. Laid up for me and shot me from cover. I never saw his face. He was a rotten shot. Or else he just meant to cripple, not kill. Whatever . . . his bullet shattered my right leg. It broke my health, I'm afraid, as well as my femur. And now they've killed O'Hearn, the real head of our resistance. He was tough, hotheaded, aggressive; he knew how to lead men, how to make them fight."

"You're too modest," Caroline said with a tinge of bitterness. "If there's a reason you can't lead, that's what it is. Fletch, Alex has done all the thinking for those people. Matthew Cordwainer doesn't want to bring on a full-scale fracas—another Lincoln County war. That would bring in a U.S. marshal, someone who'd start digging into all the particulars of this feud. So he tried another tack. He blocked access to Rincon by the Flats people."

"How could he do that?"

"With little difficulty," Alex said dryly. "He owns a wide strip of property along the east edge of town, including this end of the wagon road from the Redondo Flats. All he had to do was block it off and station a couple of Jagger's gunnies there to guard that point. So the Flats people can't obtain needed supplies from Rincon without getting shot as trespassers. That way, Cordwainer thinks, they'll be forced to abandon their claims or sell out to him for a pittance."

"That's why O'Hearn and his party were cutting that roadway out of the high country?"

"Sure. To provide a new access south of Cordwainer property. Once they reached the main road, they could freight in supplies from Vestal. You passed through it on your way here."

Doc nodded. Vestal was only an old paid-out gold camp, nearly deserted now, but it lay on the freight road that ran north from Taskerville, and it was less than a day's journey from here.

"The new road," Alex went on, "would cut accross the north edge of a national park reserve. Not exactly legal, but there's no legal way Cordwainer can block it, either."

"An illegal way, then?" Doc murmured.

"Yes . . . have one of his hired hands shoot up O'Hearn's party. But God"—Alex shook his head from side to side—"who'd have thought he'd go this far? Murder five men in cold blood?"

Doc felt an impatient burn of anger. "For Christ's sake, why do the two of you stay on here? Living in a rathole like

this, your health shot, keeping up a fight you can't win.
There must be other places, other jobs, for a man of your
skills."

The lamplight etched Alex's face with cruelly tired lines.
"Of course," he said quietly. "But Caro and I agreed at the
outset that we'd not abandon this fight, whatever happened.
We'd stick and see it out. And I told you, Fletch, these
people believe in me—as I believe in them. That sort of
confidence has to be worth something. More than words,
more than money. I think you'd agree."

Jesus, Doc thought wearily. Here it comes.

"We need help, Fletch. We need it badly, and you're a
friend. The best either of us ever had. That's part of why
Caro wrote you. The rest of it is—you're a man who can
deal powerfully with other men. Far better than either
O'Hearn or I ever could. You made your reputation, and
you lived up to it . . . until you suddenly decided to quit
that way of life—we believe because of your essential
idealism."

"Uh-huh. So?"

If Alex noted the glacial edge in Doc's voice, it failed to
dampen his quiet fervor. "Whatever your reason for turning
away from it, you've acquired uncommon skills along that
line. We didn't feel it unreasonable to suppose you might
lend those skills to a really worthy cause. It wouldn't be for
nothing, Fletch. We've made our agreement with the Flats
people. It can be renegotiated to include you. Whatever
profit Caro and I make would be half yours."

"You want me to head up a war. Is that it?"

"To provide leadership in a fight for something decent."
Alex shook his head slowly. He picked up his cold pipe and
gazed at it for a moment, then looked up, saying quietly,
"You won't do it, will you?"

"No," Doc said in a tight, savage voice. "No and no.
I've never been a damned hired gun. Never that—even at
my worst. Behind all the high-sounding crap, that's what
you're looking for—a hired gun of your own. Go to hell,
Alex. Go to hell, both of you!"

He was coming to his feet as he spoke, so quickly his chair crashed over backward. He strode to the door, wrenched it open, and slammed out of the shack. A blaze of sun hit his eyes and added to his fury. He clamped his hat on his head and started down the trail.

"Fletch . . . Fletch, wait!"

Doc kept striding furiously on but slowed his pace as Caroline's running steps neared him. Then he halted and turned. She stopped, too, recoiling a little from what she saw in his face.

"Fletch. Oh, Fletch, I'm sorry! We just didn't think. We—"

"You mean you. Wasn't it your idea to ring me in?"

"Yes." He watched the agitation wash out of her face. "Mine. But I never thought it would affect you so dreadfully. Truly I didn't."

"All right." Doc's tone was icily impersonal now. "Now you know. Five years ago I had all I could stomach of that life. I won't go back to it, Caro. Not for any reason."

"I understand."

Like hell. You were so damned sure of me.

Caroline raised her hands slightly, palms up, with a little tremulous smile. "Well, then, Fletch, that is it. What can I do? What can I say?"

She'd make Bernhardt look like the rankest of ingenues, Doc thought bitterly. But that was all right. She was doing it for a worthy cause.

"Nothing."

He turned on his heel and went on downhill. Walking away from his damned past one more time. And dully wondering if any man could ever, finally, travel that fast or that far.

CHAPTER SIX

DOC HEADED BACK FOR THE FULLER HOUSE. BUT QUARTER-ing across to it, he changed his mind and went into the noisy, roistering Shortbough Saloon alongside. It was a good match for his mood. But there was also a streak of raw red running through his thoughts. This would be a good place to feed it.

He pushed into the swirl of tobacco smoke and loud talk, the laughter and curses and badinage, the smells of smoke and sweat and strong liquor, welcoming the din and raucousness. The Shortbough was a boomtown dive and a man's hangout. It looked and sounded and stank like one. In his present mood, he welcomed all of it—the sights, the sounds, the smells.

Doc bellied up to a vacant area of the bar, feeling a little sorry there was nobody on either side he'd have to elbow away. He wouldn't have minded a minor set-to just now. Catching the bartender's eye, he signaled for whiskey— good liquor, no backbar swill—and paid for the quart of Mountain Brook that the bartender set in front of him along with a glass. He was of a mind to get as drunk as he could, a luxury he hadn't enjoyed in some time. Before pouring his first drink he picked up the glass and held it against the light to be sure it was clean. He took the drink in a quick swallow and poured another, then only stared at it.

Who did he have to blame but himself? Nobody. Hadn't he come to Rincon with more than an inkling of what the Draytons might want of him? Sure he had. Then why?

Caroline. Not a day in seventeen years had passed that he hadn't thought of her with the same dismal wrench of memory. And knowing what he would have to face, he had come, anyway; her summons, her plea for help, giving him the excuse to see her once more.

Damn you, Caroline!

He took his second drink quickly. Then a touch on his arm made him jerk around, ready for anything.

"Easy there," said Elmo Jagger. He held up his hands in a placating way, grinning to show teeth that were big and square and yellow. For some reason it made Doc think of a bared-tooth catamount. "Dr. Styles, I presume?"

That made Doc grin a little, too. "And you'd be Mr. Jagger."

Elmo Jagger inclined his head a little, still grinning. "I feel flattered, doctor. Back a while, when my boy Gregorio roughed you up, you looked familiar somehow, but I couldn't place you. Later I got thinking, and I thought, Doc Styles, sure. Saw you in Dodge City years ago. You were hanging around, sort of, with Earp and his bunch. But you were never really one of 'em. You never ran with any crowd I heard tell of."

Doc stirred his head in the negative. "I never did. But I have to own I don't remember you. Someone else just mentioned your name to me."

Jagger chuckled. "That plumb deflates me, doctor. I was quite a lot younger, just a hanger-on punk. And later on, over at Tombstone, I was with the Clanton-Behan crowd against the Earps. You and me never got to tangle horns, and I'm as glad we didn't. But look, you ain't honing to get back at Gregorio on account of that hoorawing, are you? You wasn't packing a hogleg then. I see you are now."

Again Doc shook his head. "Nothing like that, Elmo. Say it's to serve notice I won't take any more of it."

"Well, that shines. Listen, would you mind tipping that bottle over at my table?" Jagger motioned toward an unoccupied deal table in a far back corner. "I'd fancy a round of private palaver if it wouldn't discommode you a lot."

Carrying his bottle and glass, Doc followed Jagger through the mill of noisy drinkers and gamblers. Some faces were familiar: members of the gang Jagger headed up. Other patrons of the Shortbough seemed to be off-shift miners; there was a sprinkling of townsmen, too, counter-jumpers who wore black broadcloth but went informally coatless. They all mingled with a kind of freewheeling camaraderie, and you could almost fit each man into his occupation by the way he dressed and carried himself. It was the sort of easy social blend you found in a wide-open boomtown where anything might happen.

The interior of the Shortbough was pretty surprising in itself. In contrast to the drab, square-turned look of the outside building, the vast barroom had a lavish opulence that almost knocked your eye out. It was luxuriously appointed with a mahogany bar, plastered walls, some fairly tasteful paintings, and a series of matched wall lamps. Spaced at regular intervals, they relieved the windowless gloom with a mellow glow. Doc saw no roulette tables or keno goose, but several poker games, quietly cutthroat in their intensity, were going on in the midst of this racket.

Jagger motioned Doc to a chair at his small corner table where a bottle and glass already reposed. He poured a shot into Doc's glass, then his own, and raised his glass.

"*Salud*, doctor."

Doc nodded his thanks and drank. Like himself, Jagger appreciated a good whiskey. Old Crow was right up with Mountain Brook. Setting down his glass, he gave Elmo Jagger a careful and curious look-over.

Elmo was tall, bulky, wide-shouldered and, despite his
thatch of curly gray hair, was probably not much over thirty.
The lines in his square handsome face came more from hard
living than age, and among them was a dimpling of scars.
He smiled easily and often, but the humor never reached his
bleached eyes: they stayed opaque and unreadable. His
hands, toying with his glass on the table, were large and
muscular and sun-weathered, without a trace of scar or
callus. The ordinary range clothes he wore were clean and
neat, and somehow he lent them a quiet dignity. Elmo,
thought Doc, was one impressive-looking son of a bitch,
and no doubt a deadly one. It would take such a man to head
up a tough bunch of bravos.

Jagger said pleasantly, "What brings a man of your
reputation to an out-of-the-way backwater like Rincon,
doctor? I'd heard tell you had got sort of tamed in recent
times, but I wouldn't reckon there's a lot hereabouts to
claim a man of your style."

Doc smiled faintly. It wasn't uncommon in this big,
sparsely settled country for gossip about any man who'd
attracted public notice to run far ahead of him. It became
common currency around any campfire, and like as not you
knew half what there was to know about such a man before
you ever met him.

"Let's just say I needed a change of scene, Elmo. Good
enough?"

"Fine by me. Just friendly curiosity."

"People are always curious." Doc poured a drink from
his own bottle and gazed at it meditatively. "You para-
phrased Henry M. Stanley when you greeted me. I met him
once, some years back. He was writing a piece for *Harper's
Weekly* on notorious figures of the West. He had a question
for me, too."

"Not the same one?"

Doc met Jagger's mildly amused stare. "No. He wanted

to know how many men I had killed. I told him I lost count after the first dozen. Thus do legends have their genesis."

Elmo Jagger threw back his head and let out a roar of laughter that was real and appreciative. "Good, doctor. Damned good! But that whets my curiosity all over. Just how many men *have* you killed?"

Doc shook his head, grimly thinking of Thomas O'Hearn. And then, his glance moving past Jagger, he said quietly, "Let me put it this way. Number four could be tottering unsteadily toward us right now."

"Hmm?" Jagger frowned, then twisted a look over his shoulder.

The youth called Gregorio lurched up to the table, his big Californio spurs chinking loudly. He stood there swaying, his eyes glazed. "Hey, Elmo? I see you drink with Señor Four-Eyes. He mus' be some fella. You say who he is, eh?"

Jagger began to grin again. Maybe he'd like to see a ruckus kicked up. "Sure thing. Doctor, may I introduce Gregorio Ortez, better known in some quarters as the Hermosillo Kid. Gregorio, this here is Dr. Styles. John Fletcher Styles. Maybe you heard tell of him, uh?"

God, Doc thought wearily, not another Kid. In his time he'd met the Amarillo Kid, the Jicarillo kid, the plain old Rio Kid, and a host of Anglo self-styled Kids to boot. Not all of them were kids, either, but each and every one was a complete asshole.

Gregorio blinked, teetered back on his heels, then caught his balance and laughed. "Hey. I'm be a som bitch. Doc Styles, hey? Here alla time I'm think of you as ol' Four-Eyes. I'm don' think of you that way no more, pop. Hey, wha' you think a that, pop?"

"What I don't think," Doc said mildly, "is that you know cow shit from pinto beans."

"Huh?" The Hermosillo Kid swayed unsteadily, trying to focus his eyes. "Wha's that you say, pop?"

"I said, a piss ant like you is mostly good for stomping on. Only you're not half big enough for stomping, sonny."

Doc's temper was still riding a ragged edge, and now he was not only ready for trouble; he was starting to hone for it. Unlike earlier, he felt no desire to put a checkrein on the urge. Elmo Jagger, sensing that a half-playful situation was getting out of hand, quickly turned his head, calling sharply, "Hunt! Over here!"

A strapping young fellow detached himself from the rambunctious crowd at the bar and came over to their table, saying, "What's the problem, Elmo?"

"The problem is your *amigo*." Elmo jabbed a thumb at Gregorio. "Take him out of here and dunk his head in a horse trough. Anything. Just clear the mush out of his brain before you let him back in here."

"Hey, man." Gregorio was squinting hard at Doc. "Wha's that you mean about pizz ants—"

"Come on, old *amigo*." The youth called Hunt took a firm hold on Gregorio's arm and turned him. "Let's go for a walk."

Hunt was apple-cheeked, in his early twenties, and had long, silky mustachios and an impudent, easygoing grin. With his fringed buckskin trousers and bench-made Justin boots, he wore a peppermint-striped shirt and bright red sleeve garters. It was the sort of expensive, dandified getup he might have copied from the yellowback cover of any Beadle's dime novel.

"Hey, man, come on. Don' put no strong arm on me." The Hermosillo Kid tried to twist out of the hold, but Hunt effortlessly propelled him across the room to the swing doors and outside.

"Bosom pals, beyond a doubt," murmured Doc. "Who's the dude wrangler?"

"Hunt Cordwainer. Drink up, Doc."

"I will. Then I'll pour you one. Relation to Matthew Cordwainer? I hear he makes all the tracks around here."

Doc emptied his glass and then refilled his and Jagger's.

Elmo nodded his thanks. "You heard right. Hunt is old Matt's only son and the apple of his daddy's eye. Not a bad kid at all."

"He keeps sterling company, that's sure."

Jagger smiled crookedly. "The kid is young, and he's spoiled. He's out to sow his oats, and his old man is indulgent enough to let him do it with our bunch. Right now him and Gregorio are *buen compadres*. Give him time; he'll get over it."

"If he lives that long."

"You sound mighty fastidious, doctor. I mean, considering you was set to pull Gregorio's teeth a minute back. You're sort of edgy for a man who went peaceable."

"Funny, isn't it?"

"Sure is." Jagger turned his glass gently between his fingers. "Just naturally makes a man wonder if there ain't a special reason you showed up here. Course you said there ain't. No offense meant."

"None taken," Doc said idly. "What reason, for instance?"

Jagger told him about the combustible situation between the Redondo Flats people and his employer, Matthew Cordwainer. It was just a rehash of what the Draytons had already told Doc, and Jagger matter-of-factly made no effort to sugarcoat his side of it. "Crossed my mind, doctor, that the Flats folks might have decided to import a gun of their own, like you. But you gone peaceable."

"That's right. Seems I came riding into trouble here, though."

"You mean Gregorio? Hell, that's—"

"No," Doc cut in. Watching Jagger's face, he quietly told him about the murdered men he'd found.

Jagger said softly, "The devil!" His rough surprise was genuine, Doc saw. Jagger's arm had jerked in the act of pouring another drink, spilling it onto his hand. He dried the hand on his shirt, eyeing Doc narrowly. "You wouldn't feed me a string of taffy, now, would you?"

"Every word's gospel, Elmo. Go read the sign for yourself."

"No need." Jagger slumped in his chair, a tight groove of anger in his jaw. "I tell you one thing. None of us done that. Not me, not any of my boys. We're troubleshooters for hire, sure. And we ain't too choosy about our hire. But Christ, none of us is a damn butcher. Believe it or don't."

Doc believed it. And he understood another reason for Jagger's anger. Somehow Matthew Cordwainer had arranged for that butchery without Jagger's knowledge. He'd gone behind Jagger's back so to speak.

The swing doors parted. Young Hunt Cordwainer came back in, pushing Gregorio Ortez, the Hermosillo Kid, ahead of him. Hunt must have dunked Gregorio's head in a horse trough, as Jagger had advised. The kid's face was wet, his black hair dripping. He looked mean and surly as hell. He tramped over to the bar, Hunt amiably prodding him along all the way, and hollered for a drink of whiskey.

Jagger's glance shifted amusedly from Gregorio back to Doc. "Doctor, supposin' you had Gregorio for a patient, how would you diagnose a case like his?"

"As one of severe diarrhea. From the wrong end."

Again Jagger's roar of hearty laughter.

It aroused the Hermosillo Kid enough that he turned his head toward them, sluggishly and irritably. Maybe he was setting himself for another head-on with Doc. If he was, what happened next squelched the notion.

The swing doors slammed open, and Danny Mike O'Hearn stumbled in.

He was unsteady on his feet, reeling a little as if dizzy. But he was boiling with anger; his face twisted with it. He came to a stop, legs braced apart, eyes wild, hands half curled into fists.

"Which of you bloody bastards done it?" he yelled. "You killed my brother. You killed our friends. Which one of you bastards done it?"

CHAPTER SEVEN

THE KID MUST HAVE COME OUT OF HIS STATE OF CONCUSSION a lot faster than Doc had figured he would. That happened sometimes. He was seething with rage, and Dr. Kroll had probably had no choice but to tell him what Doc had told Kroll.

Now Danny Mike was crazed with grief and out for blood. Only any blood that got shed was likely to be his. Doc groaned inwardly. *Is that what I saved this redheaded bogtrotter's neck for?*

The room had dropped into silence, and now men began muttering and shifting their feet. From the middle of the bar the Hermosillo Kid eyed Danny Mike in a cold, wicked, measuring way and then spoke up.

"Gringo. Hey. I'm the one done for your brother. What you going to do about it? Huh?"

Elmo Jagger said quietly, "Goddam it," then raised his voice warningly. "Gregorio! No more of that. Leave it alone, you hear?"

"Hey, man, no, I'm leave nothing alone. This gringo ridge runner, he wan' a fight. Okay, then he fight me."

Gregorio didn't even glance at Jagger as he spoke. He swallowed a whiskey and banged his glass down on the bar.

48

Wild for trouble, any kind of trouble, he leaned negligently against the bar, smiling, watching young O'Hearn.

Danny Mike moved forward across the room. He was stocky and strong, and he looked mean enough to take on tigers. But he was unarmed, and he took slow, uncertain steps, still woozy from his wound.

Nobody moved; nobody said a word. The Hermosillo Kid just grinned and waited. When Danny Mike reached him and made an awkward grab for him, Gregorio stepped away with a mocking laugh. Then he brought up a fist and brought it down, like a carpenter driving nails.

The blow caught Danny Mike behind the left ear. He pitched to the floor, falling on his face.

Gregorio laughed again, then bent and caught a fistful of Danny Mike's collar and hoisted up the boy's head till their faces were inches apart.

"Listen, you silly-ass shit. You wan' a fight, huh? Okay, we fight. You *borracho* like me, but maybe can hold a gun, huh? You ain' got a gun, you get one. You better find one real quick, *muchacho*. You better find one inside five minutes. 'Cause tha's when I be back. You ain' ready then, man, you know what I do? I shoot you cold turkey."

Gregorio let go of Danny Mike and, spurs chinking, walked slowly to the swing doors. Slowly, because he wanted to show how cocksure he was but also because, though partly sobered, he had too much liquor in his system to manage a faster walk.

The swing doors rocked shut behind him. Hunt Cordwainer made a move as if to follow him, then slacked back against the bar, shaking his head.

Danny Mike O'Hearn climbed to his feet, scrubbing a hand over his skinned face, wiping a finger under his bloody nose. He clutched at the bar for support.

Christ's mercy, thought Doc. *Here you go again. All right.* He shoved back his chair and got to his feet. Then he picked up his bottle and glass and started toward the bar.

"Doctor." Elmo Jagger spoke very softly, and Doc paused and glanced at him. Jagger wasn't smiling now. "I wouldn't mix in this if I was you."

Doc gave him a near-pleasant grin. "Only you're not. I've enjoyed our little chat, Elmo. But I've a word of advice for you, too."

Jagger's big yellow teeth showed, still not smiling. "I can guess. Stay out of your way."

"Elmo, you're way ahead of me." Doc paused. "That's part of it. The rest is, you stay out front. Don't you or any of your lads get moving around back of me. I wouldn't like it a bit."

He walked around behind the bar, set his bottle and glass on it, then peered underneath. On a shelf he found what he'd half expected: a sawed-off Greener shotgun. Quite a few barmen kept them on hand for quelling riots or putting down potential trouble. Doc picked up the shotgun, blew the dust off it, and half broke the gun till he saw the brass rims of the two double-aught shotshells it contained.

He snapped the breech shut. The sound brought the bartender out of a frozen reverie. He was young and skinny and freckled and, Doc guessed, very new to his job. He said, "Hey, you can't do that!"

"Only I did. What you do, sonny, is you stand away and stay quiet. Throw your apron over your head if you want. That way you never saw a damn thing."

The young bartender wasn't the only one who'd been caught off guard by the Hermosillo Kid's sudden challenge. All the games and drinking had ceased, and now every man's attention was on Doc. He stepped out from behind the bar, went over to Danny Mike O'Hearn, and said mildly, "Well, Red. You dealt yourself into a nice tight jackpot."

Danny Mike was leaning both hands against the bar to hold himself upright. He shook his head slowly back and forth, looking woozily at Doc. A slight beard fuzzed his jaws, and his eyes were wild and bloodshot. Blood was dribbling from his nose; he licked it off his upper lip.

"Who'n hell are you?" he asked thickly.

"The man who brought you in. I saved your bacon once, and there's an outside chance maybe I can again. Only you hear me out."

Tucking the shotgun under one arm, Doc poured a drink from his bottle. He handed the glass to Danny Mike. "Swallow that and listen to me."

The kid blinked twice. Half angrily, he opened his mouth and then closed it. Then took the drink in a gulp. Doc poured him another, said, "Take this one slowly," and then eased the shotgun to a casual aim on the room at large. "You hear what he said? Did you get it all straight?" he asked the boy.

"I got it."

"Fine. You've got choices. Clear out before he comes back. Or—"

"I ain't running from no dry-gulching son of a bitch!" the kid said hotly.

"No," Doc said wearily. "You won't do that, Red, will you? Got to keep that old pecker right up there. All right. He's a gun tipper, but he's also half drunk. Not much of an edge, but it's about all you have."

Danny Mike stared at him muddily. Doc pulled his Navy Colt from the shoulder holster and said, "Take it." Danny Mike did, hesitantly and awkwardly. Sweet God a'mighty, Doc thought sinkingly. Has he ever even held a hogleg? He kept his voice calm and mild. "Pay attention. Get every word I tell you. There won't be time to say it again."

Doc took the gun back and talked quietly, trying to distill into a few minutes what it had taken him many hours to come by. A couple of times, illustrating the points he was getting at about bringing a pistol to level, holding on a target, getting a shot off, he passed the gun to the kid and took it back again.

All the while he kept half his attention on the roomful of men, particularly Elmo Jagger. But Jagger was slumped in his chair, looking relaxed and sleepily amused. So long as

Doc wasn't taking a personal hand other than offering advice, he was willing to go along. Why not? Doc could taste a bleak hopelessness in his own interference.

Passing the Navy Colt back to Danny Mike a last time, he said, "Now you're up for it, kid. Try to do what I told you. And for Christ's sake, *take your time*."

The kid tossed off the rest of his drink and turned enough to face the swing doors straight on. Doc moved off out of line, holding the shotgun negligently under his arm. A chance in a hundred? Maybe better. The boy was steady, ramrod-straight, the color back in his face.

In less than a half minute the Hermosillo Kid came through the doors, banging them back hard on their rockers. He must have dunked his head again; his hair was freshly wet, his gaze darting and wicked.

"Well," he said in almost a velvety tone, "so you are loaning a hand, pop, huh? Tha's it?"

Doc shook his head. "Game's all yours and his. All I'm lending is a little insurance."

"Insurance? Wha's that for, huh?"

"Ask your boss."

Gregorio gave a soft, contemptuous chuckle. "Your insurance, it don' do this gringo *chingado* no good, pop—"

He was moving deeper into the room as he spoke, his hand dipping and now coming up with a heavy Army Colt lifted from a cutaway holster. You needn't be a fast-draw artist if your gun was already out, Doc had matter-of-factly told Danny Mike, and young O'Hearn was holding Doc's Navy Colt down by his side.

Now he brought it up in an easy motion as Doc had told him to, holding it out and pointing it as a man might point a finger. Later Doc would remember how coolly and naturally he did it.

Then there was only the slam of gun roar as the Hermosillo Kid kept moving forward, cat-crouched, fanning his shots off, batting the lower edge of his left palm against the hammer of his heavy Colt.

He got off four shots in a continuous din of sound, dirty white powder smoke shrouding ahead of him, and every one sprayed wide of its mark. Doc felt a fleeting relief at his own wisdom in having moved well out of the line of fire. For Gregorio was the silly-ass shit he had named Danny Mike.

Gunfanning was all right if you were sitting at a gambling table across from someone who'd taken enough exception to your play that he pulled iron on you. Get your own piece out first and fan off one shot at him from maybe a yard away, you had him cold. But no man alive, standing more than thirty feet from his target and fanning off his shots, could hit anything smaller than a barn door except by accident.

Danny Mike held the Navy Colt easily pointed, and he shot just once.

The Hermosillo Kid was stopped in his tracks like an axed steer and then flung backward by the full impact of a bullet in the middle of his chest. He crashed to the splintered floor and his body skidded maybe a foot through the dry scatter of sawdust and came to a stop with arms outflung, oddly like a man crucified.

Doc was already moving toward young O'Hearn, taking his gun quickly back from the boy's drooping fist. Danny Mike had grimaced and grunted hard as Gregorio had pulled off his fifth shot, firing at the same time young O'Hearn did. And now, Doc saw, the whole right thigh of Danny Mike's pants was drenched with a wet darkness. He was slumping downward now, both hands grabbing at his wounded thigh.

One-armed, Doc rammed his Navy Colt into its holster and caught Danny Mike around the shoulders to hold him up while his right hand kept the Greener trained on the room.

Hunt Cordwainer was the only one who moved. He tramped over to the Hermosillo Kid and dropped on one knee beside him, then touched his chest, as if not believing this. He looked up, his face wild with grief and rage. His buddy, Doc thought. Too bad, but a man ought to choose his friends better.

"We're going out of here," said Doc into a silence that reeked of burned powder. "Both of us. Anyone objects and wishes to say so, I will be pleased to blow his head off his shoulders."

The words were a gesture, theatrical bombast of the sort you felt obliged to come out with at crucial times. Even if you meant what you said, you felt like a damned histrionic fool saying it.

But everyone outside of Elmo Jagger seemed to take it seriously. Jagger was still slack in his chair, his shoulders faintly shaking. Was the son of a bitch laughing straight-faced? Sure he was. They understood each other so well Jagger could find it humorous even now. The son of a bitch was as hard as a railroad spike, and Doc felt a flicker of angry admiration.

He tossed the shotgun on the bar and pulled out his shoulder gun again, keeping it ready as he backed away toward the swing doors, holding the half-conscious boy upright. At the doors he half turned to shoulder his way through them, looking out to check the street, and in that instant Jagger yelled warningly, *"Hunt!"*

Doc swung his head around, thumbing the Navy Colt on cock. Hunt Cordwainer had come suddenly to his feet, hand wrapped around the butt of his side-holstered pistol.

Nothing else happened. Jagger's shout had broken the moment. Hunt let his hand fall and settled back on his heels, his young face still working crazily. Doc pushed out through the doors and stepped aside fast.

Nobody followed.

CHAPTER EIGHT

THE GUNFIRE INSIDE THE SHORTBOUGH HADN'T ATTRACTED much attention outside. In a hard-rock camp like Rincon, shooting fracases were common; quite often, too, cutups would shoot off their guns for the hell of it. A few mildly curious glances were all that Doc drew as he edged down one side of the street between the porches and the tie rails, holding up Danny Mike O'Hearn.

The kid was chunkily built and almost a dead weight, his feet dragging, chin slumped on his chest. Moreover, Doc had to slog through deep mud and keep looking back to be sure none of Jagger's toughs was coming after him. The strain on his muscles and patience kept him swearing steadily, if silently, all the way to the foot of the outside stairway that led to Dr. Kroll's second-story office.

Doc eased Danny Mike down onto the bottom risers and tramped up to the office door. He'd raised his fist to hammer on it when he saw the pasteboard sign hanging from the door latch: OUT ON CALL.

Now he swore out loud, viciously and at some length.

Having gotten that much out of his system, he descended the stairway, hauled Danny Mike up, and used what felt like his last residue of strength getting him over to the livery barn and inside, dumping him on a bed of hay in an unoccupied horse stall.

By now the kid's whole pants leg and boot were blood-soaked. Doc ripped off the boot and with his pocketknife slashed the pants leg from hip to knee. The wound was a couple of inches above the knee and bleeding freely, and as far as Doc could tell from a cursory look, the bone hadn't been touched. But the bullet hadn't emerged; it was lodged somewhere in the fleshy part of the thigh.

Squatting on his haunches, Doc scrubbed a palm over his whisker-furred jaws. He'd fix this hothead bogtrotter's leg as well as he could. Then he'd get him the hell out of a town that held nothing but people who'd be indifferent to his plight if they weren't plain-out enemies and get him back in the hands of his friends.

Doc swore again savagely. If only there was someone else to handle the job. He was already neck-deep in the sort of jackpot he'd sworn off years ago. Meantime, every damned move he'd made, evasive or altruistic, had only served to pull him in deeper.

"Uh, hey, mister . . ."

Doc spun on his heels. Given the wicked run of his thoughts just now, he was in no mood for even a diffident interruption of them. "What is it?" he snarled at the elderly, rheumy-eyed hostler.

"I, uh, nothing, sir. Just can I help you anyways atall?"

Doc stood up, brushing wisps of hay from his trousers. "You might. Do you have any rigs for hire? A spring wagon?"

The hostler allowed he did. Doc told him to hitch one up to a good team and to saddle up Doc's own mount. Afterward Doc crossed swiftly to the Fuller House, went up to his room, collected his belongings, and returned to the barn. With the quick dexterity of practice, of longtime improvising, he cut and tore his other shirt into strips. One of them he twisted into a ropelike tourniquet that he knotted above the kid's thigh wound to check the bleeding; he also fashioned a rough bandage. The remaining strips of cloth he rammed into his pocket.

Get out of here fast! It was the sole and urgent thought that occupied Doc as he and the hostler lifted Danny Mike O'Hearn into the bed of the spring wagon after laying down a pallet of hay to cushion the boy's body.

"You know the road that leads up to the Redondo Flats?" Doc asked the hostler.

"Yes, sir. But you'll have the pluperfect hell of a time getting up it, that's what you got in mind. There's a couple of—"

"I know. Just get me headed onto it. You know where the O'Hearn place is?"

"No, sir. But 'low that anyone up on the Flats can tell you."

With his own mount tied to the wagon tailgate, Doc lifted the team into a brisk trot toward the east edge of town. With no difficulty, he found the road there and followed its switchbacking loops into the heights above Rincon. In spite of his half-understanding with Jagger, he looked back often for any sign of pursuit.

None was in sight by the time he reached the barrier that Matthew Cordwainer had laid on the east flank of his land. Sizable boulders had been rolled across the road, and a couple of armed men were sprawled in the shade of a bough-thatched lean-to. They got up and stepped out, rifles in hand, as Doc pulled up the wagon.

The younger man said, "Best you turn that rig back, mister. Nobody gets through here. Orders from the property owner."

"As I understand it," Doc said mildly, "your orders are to turn back anyone coming from the *other* way."

"More or less, that's it. Long as there's no grub supplies in that wagon."

"Just a hurt man I'm taking home to his folks. Have a look for yourselves."

They did. The younger guard glanced questioningly at
the older one, who shrugged and said, "Reckon it'll do to
let 'em through."

"Obliged," Doc said. "You fellows mind helping me
move a few rocks so I can slip the wagon around?"

The two guards lent a hand, rolling a couple of large
rocks at one end of the barrier aside, creating a space that
enabled Doc to rein through on the road shoulder. He
thanked the men and drove on. His hands were sweating
around the reins, for he hadn't been sure what to expect
when he came up against Matthew Cordwainer's roadblock.

It was a long but pleasant drive along the winding dusty
road up the pine-clad slopes to the Redondo Flats. Hazy
slats of sunlight cut through the boughs of tall lodgepole
pines that crowded next to the road; they made a greenish
glow of quiet light all around. Squirrels chattered; insects
buzzed in the sun shafts.

All the same, Doc kept alert. One of Jagger's toughs was
dead, and at least one of the rest, young Cordwainer, was in
a seething rage.

Doc made frequent stops to check on Danny Mike's
condition. Already weakened by the bullet crease in his
head—it had bled a little more but not much—the kid
seemed to have gone into shock from the fresh wound. Doc
alternately loosened and tightened the leg tourniquet for the
sake of circulation, and once he changed the blood-soaked
bandages. By now the bleeding had lessened quite a bit, and
he thought the kid should make it through. But Danny Mike
looked an awful mess, pale and unconscious, his hair and
clothes matted with dried blood.

As the road climbed out of the forested range into the off-
tapering flats above it, Doc began to feel a small prickling
of flesh at the back of his neck. Sometimes that particular
feeling was a result of nerves. But not always. Having
heeded several such premonitions in the past, he was
convinced that on occasion they'd saved his life.

Where the road made a sharp turn on a stony height of land, Doc halted the team and wagon in the cover of a deep niche of boulders. He stepped to the ground and pulled his rifle and field glasses out of his gear. Then he climbed up on a spur of rock topped by some scrub grass and stretched out on his belly. He leveled the glasses on the long down-slant of his backtrail, sweeping them slowly across wherever he could spot stretches of road between the clumps of trees and brush and boulders.

For a full minute he made out nothing at all. Then his glasses tracked across a flashing wink of reflected sun that made him swing them back to bear on that glimmer. It vanished suddenly, moving forward and cut off abruptly by intervening boulders. Doc moved his sights to the open stretch of road just ahead of the boulders. He tightened his focus and waited.

Three riders, jogging into sight one by one.

The man in the lead was young Cordwainer. The sun flash had come from the band of silver *conchas* he wore on his Stetson. What of the men behind him? Doc had vague memories of their faces: two others of Jagger's bunch, and hardly more than kids.

Jagger himself, Doc was almost dead sure, knew nothing about it. Elmo would have his own rough code about such a thing. It had been an even break between his man and Danny Mike O'Hearn. One had to lose; let it go at that. Hunt Cordwainer wouldn't be so philosophical. Danny Mike had killed his good friend, and Doc Styles had lent a hand. The other two? Also pals of Gregorio Ortez, or they were just young and reckless enough to follow Hunt's lead.

Stop them cold, thought Doc. Short of killing if you can. But stop 'em soon or they'll have both our asses in a basket.

A sharp groan came from the wagon. He looked quickly back and saw that Danny Mike was stirring on his bed of hay, twisting his legs, flinging a bent arm across his face.

For the moment he was partly conscious. Maybe enough to
give out vital information.

Doc scanned the three riders again. They were coming on
steadily but slowly, obviously wary of ambush, and they
were still several hundred yards and many minutes short of
this point. All right.

He scrambled down from the rock and went to the
wagon. He got out his canteen, uncapped it, and, lifting
Danny Mike's shoulders, tipped it to his parched lips. The
boy gulped greedily. His head rolled back, and he regarded
Doc with glazed, fevered eyes.

"You're—"

"Dr. John Fletcher Styles."

"The man who saved my bacon. Sure."

Doc almost smiled. The kid remembered him from the
Shortbough. Could even dredge up a touch of humor,
echoing Doc's own phrase. But his voice was frail and
whispery.

"I saved it twice," said Doc. "You got the Hermosillo
Kid. Got him dead. But he got you, too. Remember that?"

Young O'Hearn dipped his chin in affirmation.

"Now I'm trying to get you home. Can you help me?"

Danny Mike squinted up puzzledly at the sky. "Where
are we?"

Doc described their present situation as well as he could,
briefly. Danny Mike was in bad shape, but momentarily he
had enough awareness to sketch out faltering directions to
where the O'Hearn place was located, over on the south
flank of the Redondo Flats where they shouldered almost
against a sharp lift of the Sweetwater range. He got in a few
more details, as well, and then, abruptly, his eyes closed,
his head tipping sideways.

Doc felt for his pulse. Strong and steady. But Danny
Mike had used up all he had for just now.

Climbing back onto the rock spur, stretching out flat
again, Doc got Hunt and his pals back into focus. They

were just about inside good rifle range, but he wanted them in a wide open space before he put a strong message across to them.

Now, he thought. The three were crossing a stretch of bare rock with hardly any cover available for yards around. Doc nestled his .45–.70 Winchester to his shoulder, thumbed the hammer to full cock, and carefully squeezed off his shot.

It kicked up rock dust so close to the feet of young Cordwainer's sorrel that the animal shied away, reared up, and came down, fiddle-footing wildly. Levering fresh cartridges into the chamber as fast as he could, Doc fired them off as quickly as his hasty aiming would permit, putting more screaming ricochets close to the horses' feet.

The animals were in complete panic, rearing and plunging. Hunt and his companions tried to hold them down on tight reins and couldn't. Giving it up, they piled off their mounts in a hurry, at the same time yanking their carbines from saddle scabbards and running for the nearest cluster of rocks. Doc hurried them along by laying more shots close to their heels.

Hunt stumbled and slammed down on his belly, losing his grip on his carbine. It skidded far out of his reach. His nerve broke; he scrambled back to his feet and dived behind the rock cluster where his two buddies had taken refuge.

Doc smiled, coughing against the reek of cordite fumes that hung in the sun-hot stillness. As the stink of powder smoke faded, he began digging more shells out of his pocket, preparatory to reloading.

Suddenly, Hunt Cordwainer, shamed by his show of panic, lunged out of the rocks and ran to retrieve his abandoned carbine. Doc swore quietly. In the back of his mind he'd methodically counted the shots he'd squeezed off and knew that his fifteen-shot magazine contained one last cartridge. He levered the Winchester, and just as Hunt bent to seize hold of his weapon, fired.

He'd meant to place the shot between Hunt's hand and the weapon, but in his haste pulled a trifle high. Hunt screamed and fell to the ground, writhing, grabbing at an arm. His two friends, heedless of any risk to themselves, rushed out and lifted him up, one on either side, and dragged him back to cover.

Mechanically, Doc reloaded his Winchester. But he didn't fire again, not even to spook them.

He felt sick and shaken once more, almost as much as when his bullet had cut down Thomas O'Hearn. Maybe only a gunman or a physician could appreciate the god-awful mess made by a lead pellet tearing into live flesh. And into bone, sinew, nerves, blood vessels. Only a gunman or a physician. And he was both.

But it was done. And so, he guessed, was any pursuit by these three. Now they'd have to catch their horses and get Hunt back to town and whatever medical care was available.

CHAPTER NINE

DOC MADE HIS WAY SLOWLY THROUGH THE SHIMMERING heat of midday and into the late afternoon. Heat reflecting from naked rocks, from the direct rays of a down-beating sun, baked and broiled a man to the bone. All the same, Doc drove the wagon slowly. He wanted to spare the wounded boy any needless punishment, not push the horses too hard, and take his bearings carefully so as not to miss any of the landmarks or trail turns that Danny Mike had described.

He crossed a good piece of the Redondo Flats during that time. The meandering traces along which he guided the wagon were, he guessed, originally old trails worn into the land by game animals and Indians. The wagon ruts of more recent years hardly showed on the arid earth.

Persecuted by the big Anglo landowners, the Mexicans who inhabited the flats must have found them a welcome place of refuge; there was little else to recommend them. Broad patches of grass here and there, with cattle grazing on them, were broken by clay dunes and rotted spires of granite caprock. The scars of erosion from wind and water showed everywhere. Doc guessed, from the many dry arroyos he had to work the wagon across or around, that there was heavy drainage off the mountain heights from spring meltwater and summer storms. They would come and pass quickly, leaving the terrain badly watered most of the year around. And there would be almost no water at all, once the mine shafts tapped by Alex's tunneling, and his successor's, had done all their work. Most of the grass, moreover, was wiry bunchgrass and tough grama that would barely support the gaunt-ribbed cattle he saw.

A tough-luck piece of country for sure. The kind that only a hardscrabble bunch of people driven into a corner were likely to take up living on. Depending on your turn of mind, you might feel either pity or contempt for such people. But you were almost bound to admire their instinct for survival, their streak of pure guts.

None of the outfits on the Redondo Flats could be very sizable ones. Picking his way along the intersecting trails, Doc had a chance to size up some of the dwellings and outsheds from a distance. None, as far as he could tell, was surrounded by more than a few hundred acres of grazing land, and he supposed the families that owned them eked out a living as much from growing crops on a few acres as from all the cattle ranging across the rest of their range.

Doc, unfamiliar with the country, had to make his way slowly, stopping often to check on Danny Mike's condition. Night drew on, and the light faded from the sky. Doc was numb and weary and in a totally foul state of mind when finally, just after early dark closed down, he picked out a couple of squares of light ahead. Lamplit windows of a house. If he'd followed Danny Mike's directions anywhere near right, this had to be the O'Hearn place.

What might he expect?

Danny Mike had gotten out that his brother had a wife—widowed now—and a daughter, and there was Tom's wife's brother, who was "kind of a great big dummy." That was the family and crew of this outfit, along with Danny Mike and his late brother. And there was the dog, old Tigre; better watch out for the dog if he wasn't tied up, Danny Mike had whispered just before he'd passed out.

So Doc went forward carefully as the last dusk ebbed into violet darkness. Just a sliver of moon now topping the Sweetwaters gave him enough light to make out his way. He was still a good distance from the squat box of a house and the dark shapes of a few outbuildings when the dog picked him up and started a wild barking.

The racket put an edge to Doc's nerves, and he checked the team short of the ranch yard. He couldn't see the dog, but he must be tethered close by; all the barking came from one spot, off in the darkness to Doc's left. Doc eased the weight of his Navy Colt in its shoulder holster and swung down off the wagon seat. He walked slowly toward the house and had just opened his mouth to hail its occupants when he caught a fleeting movement from the corner of his eye.

His hand flicked to his gun butt even before he began to turn, but too late. He was seized from behind by someone who, from the feel of him, was big and solid and powerful. The hands that gripped his arms, immobilizing them, were ham-huge, as strong as iron clamps. He was like a baby in the hands of a giant, he realized, and didn't bother to struggle.

He waited, trying to relax against the giant's terrible grip.

In a moment the door of the house opened. Light from the small windows on either side was augmented by a full spill of lamplight from the rectangle of the open doorway. The tall figure of a woman was outlined there.

"Bernardo?" she said sharply. "*Qué pasa?*"

The hulk of a man holding Doc rumbled a reply of sorts. He had a speech impediment of some kind; Doc could tell that much at once. Quite often, he knew, people who were close to one so afflicted could make out his words easily where strangers couldn't. That could be the case here.

"*Creo que sí,*" the woman said calmly, adding in the purest Spanish, "Bring this man into the house, Bernardo. Then we'll see what's to be done."

The powerful hands urged him forward, into the long throw of light from the door, and then inside the house.

The woman stepped aside as they entered, then reached out to lift Doc's Navy Colt from the shoulder rig. "*Habla español*, señor?"

"Yes," Doc replied in Spanish. "Reasonably well."

"*Bueno*. Why have you come here?"

"To bring an injured man home. He is Danny Mike O'Hearn. The brother of your late husband—if you're Mrs. O'Hearn?"

"Danny?" The planes of her handsome face changed slightly. "You have brought him here? He is alive?"

"Yes. Alive but hurt. He's in the wagon outside."

The woman spoke briefly to Bernardo, telling him to let go of Doc, but she did not give back Doc's gun. "Then we will bring him in."

She turned to a girl standing behind her, a girl of twelve or thirteen. "Biddie, go turn back the blankets of Danny Mike's bed. *Andale!*"

Bernardo, Doc saw as he turned sideways now to face his captor, was a mountainous slab of muscle, huge-shouldered and ugly as sin. He stood six or seven inches above six feet, and his face might have been hewn from brown granite, with an exaggeratedly jutting and prognathous jaw. In his worn vaquero's outfit, Bernardo looked big enough to take on a pack of wolves and whip the daylights out of the whole pack one-handed. If this was Mrs. O'Hearn's brother, she'd hardly need worry about personal protection despite her recent widowhood.

She lifted the coal-oil lamp from the table, and Doc led the way out to the wagon, closely followed by her and the hulking Bernardo. Doc and Bernardo lifted Danny Mike out of the wagon bed and carried him into the house and through to a small room at the rear. The girl, Biddie, had thrown back the blankets of a narrow cot; they eased him onto it.

Only now did Mrs. O'Hearn speak again. "What happened to him?"

Feeling a weary bite of irritation, Doc told the story one more time, again leaving out that he had killed Thomas O'Hearn. Right here, of all places, he wasn't about to disclose that.

Mrs. O'Hearn watched him impassively as he talked.

She was a damned handsome woman, Doc thought, meeting her gaze straight on. Not classically beautiful by any means. But classic standards of beauty wouldn't allow for the sharply chiseled strength of her face, with its broad, high cheekbones and the black brows ruled almost pencil-straight above hawklike eyes that swept him with a swift, merciless scrutiny. She was as tall as Doc, eyeing him on an equal level, and her skin—like her brother's—was so dusky brown that he guessed her blood heritage was almost wholly Indian. Her costume was Mexican in the traditional peasant way: a loose, scoop-necked blouse, a full skirt that left the ankles bare, and rope-soled sandals on naked feet. The body it enclosed was shapely in a kind of lean, muscular way.

"So, then . . ."

She lowered the lamp, which she'd still held high as he spoke, as if to better study his face. "That is what we found," she said matter-of-factly. "When my husband and the others did not return last night or early today, a search party went out. We found the bodies of all except Danny Mike. And you have brought him to us. *Gracias*. I am Ana O'Hearn. And this is my brother, Bernardo Martinez."

She smiled very faintly, and Doc knew that whatever grief she felt at her husband's passing was buried, locked from an outsider's view.

"John Fletcher Styles." He inclined his head slightly. "I believe I have mentioned that I'm a physician and I think it's time I examined your brother-in-law's injuries again."

Ana held the lamp close as he studied Danny Mike's scalp crease, which appeared to have begun a clean healing. The thigh wound was another matter. The Hermosillo Kid's bullet was still buried somewhere in the flesh, and Doc could only speculate on its probable depth and the angle of penetration. Maybe, going only on guesswork, he should leave it to encyst. But he decided instead to try extracting it.

Water was boiled, a jackknife blade immersed in it, and a piece of clean and worn cloth was torn up for more bandages. Doc went to work, making an incision toward where he judged an exit wound would be if the bullet's force hadn't been spent before it could emerge. He had no laudanum, no ether, no scalpel, no forceps, no proper surgical amenities of any kind. All he could do was dig around, feel his way gradually, and even do a little praying, which he hadn't done at all since Gettysburg.

It was a long and touchy and bloody job. Danny Mike was in fever now, his body jerking convulsively, and he made incoherent noises. Doc couldn't have managed except for Bernardo's mighty hands gripping Danny Mike's body tightly, holding him down flat and more or less immobile. Ana's steady hand held the lamp next to Doc's hands or moved it a little as he directed her.

Doc's guess was fairly near the mark. The lead slug lay close to skin surface. It popped free in a sudden gout of blood, as if the mutilated tissue behind were straining it outward. All that remained, at least all that he could manage, was to do a little stitching with needle and thread supplied from Ana's sewing basket and then apply bandages.

When it was over and he'd helped Ana and Biddie clean up the mess left by this primitive surgery, Doc felt sweated dry. He didn't even think to ask for the return of his Navy Colt, but Ana silently handed it back to him.

All of them went back to the common room at the front, and Ana told Doc to sit down while she made some coffee. He seated himself at the long scarred table, and so did Bernardo and the girl. Bernardo, his great spatulate hands folded on the table in front of him, eyed Doc steadily but dully, like the great dim-witted oaf he appeared to be. Biddie watched Doc with a quiet curiosity that held no judgment.

Doc glanced around the room. As this was high, well-timbered country, the house was built of logs rather than the adobe of lowland Mexican dwellings to which he was more accustomed. Yet it reminded him strongly of them. The house had one story and was low ceilinged. He saw a water *olla* that was hung from a rafter to keep it cool. From other rafters were strung chains of peppers. The whole room was an odd but pleasing mixture of Mexican and Anglo-Irish furnishings and decorations.

Doc felt dead weary, but he made an effort to be pleasant. "Biddie," he said. "Is that short for Bridget?"

"I guess so," the girl said in acceptable English. "Pa told me it was." Dark smudges of strain showed under her eyes, and the eyes themselves were reddened. She must have done a lot of crying not long since. "He was Irish. He gave me the name."

Doc nodded. She was a very pretty girl, rather tall for her age, still built along the lanky coltish lines of childhood. She was dressed in the same manner as her mother, but her skin had a lighter tone. A burnish of Irish auburn ran through the dark hair that fell loosely down her back.

"Here is the coffee," said Ana, setting a steaming cup in front of Doc. "Would you like something with it, doctor? We have some tequila. Or . . . a little whiskey?"

"Excellent thought, señora. Tequila will do very well. *Mil gracias*."

Doc gratefully sipped the tequila-laced coffee. Ana served straight coffee to her brother and daughter and then seated herself at the table. Her glance at Doc, still shutting off the wells of her grief, held only friendly curiosity.

"Thank you for doing what you have done. You can have no interest in our troubles."

Doc sipped his coffee again. "I sort of got worked into
it."

Ana smiled. "Yes. I think so, from what you have said.
You speak our language very well for an Anglo."

Doc grinned with a corner of his mouth. "Border Mex."

"No. You speak the true Spanish."

"So do you. Do you speak English? *Habla inglés?*"

"I have a little, *sí*." She spoke haltingly in English. "But
I don't do it good at all. Tomás, he always try to teach me. I
never do it good."

"*Por nada.*" Doc promptly switched back to Spanish.
"One needs but a single language if one speaks it well."

"But you are a man of true learning," said Ana. "I think
I have never met such a man."

"There are different sorts of knowing, señora. And most
of the best does not come from studying books. It comes
from living."

"If you say, it is so." She returned the smile. "Will you
remain the night? There is an extra bunk in Bernardo's
cabin."

"*Gracias.* I will tend my horses if you'll tell me where
your corral or stable is."

Ana shook her head. "No. I see you are very tired.
Bernardo will do that. A little more coffee and tequila,
doctor?"

Doc nodded sleepily, not arguing.

He'd accept the proffered hospitality and be away from
here early tomorrow. Make a brief stop in Rincon to return
the team and wagon to the livery barn. Then he would head
back for Taskerville with a free conscience, the trouble
behind him.

That's all he wanted now.

CHAPTER TEN

BERNARDO'S QUARTERS WERE IN A CRUDE ONE-ROOM LOG cabin set off east of the main house. The big man showed Doc the way there, guiding him with a lantern and carrying an armload of clean bedding provided by Ana. The spare bunk she'd mentioned was a pole-frame platform built into one corner. Against Doc's mild suggestions that he not trouble himself, Bernardo arranged the bedclothes on the bunk, his great crooked hands adjusting the blankets with the precision of any chambermaid. Doc paused only long enough to shuck off his coat and boots before collapsing onto the blankets in a dreamless sleep.

Sometime in the night he was awakened by the urgency of a hand gripping his shoulder, shaking him. "Doctor, wake up!"

Doc rolled over groggily, blinking at the flare of a lantern in Ana's high-held fist. "Wha's it?"

"It is Danny. *Por favor,* can you come quick? He's out of his head."

Doc yanked on his boots and stumbled after her to the main house. Danny Mike, he found, was running a high fever. He was throwing himself back and forth, raving incoherently. He'd burst open his bandages and was bleeding severely.

Doc took heroic measures. With Ana's and Bernardo's

help in holding the boy down, he removed the soaked wrappings and checked the bleeding by coating the wound with some bluestone Ana found in a cupboard. They applied fresh bandages, then tied Danny Mike's wrists and ankles to the corners of the bunk with cut-up lengths of rawhide catch-rope.

Afterward Doc stepped back and slowly ran a sleeve across his sweating face. It was a rotten way to restrain a man in fever, but what choice did he have? No laudanum. No ether. Nothing to subdue the kid's thrashings.

And no quinine to reduce the fever. That's what Danny Mike really needed.

For a long minute Doc was wrenched between his desire to clear out of the country as soon as he'd planned and his reluctance to desert a sick man. He had saved this dumbhead kid's life twice, and now he was treating him as a patient. It amounted to a commitment of sorts.

And Doc felt himself filled with a bleak and bitter conviction that he couldn't deny no matter how much he might wish to. Tomorrow, he knew, he would return to Rincon and obtain the necessary medication from Dr. Kroll and come back to Redondo Flats and see that the dumbhead kid was properly administered to until he got well or died.

Jesus, he thought wearily, what do you call that? Code of hypocrites?

Doc caught a couple more hours of sleep. Before daybreak, he was on his way to Rincon, driving the rented wagon with his bay gelding tied behind. The sun was high when he came to the roadblock, and he approached it slowly. Both guards were on their feet, rifles in hand, watching him warily but making no threatening move.

Doc pulled the wagon to a halt. "You get told about me?" he asked mildly.

The older man spat sideways across his arm. "We got told. Jagger sent a man. You're Doc Styles."

"Uh-huh. He send you any orders, too?"

"Just said to watch out for you. No real orders." The guard eyed him carefully. "Not less'n you aim to fetch back any grub supplies. That order stands."

"No food. Just some medicine. For the hurt boy."

"That's good." The guard spat again. "Go right on through."

Doc gauged their attitudes, decided it was all right, and then reined around the barrier and past it. All the same, he kept his head half turned, watching both guards out of the corner of his eye till he was out of sight around a crook in the road.

Rincon was the same noisy workaday cauldron of activity it had been the day before. This was a Sunday, but there was no concession to Sabbath peace. Doc fought his way through the roiling traffic to the livery barn and left the rented wagon and team there. Afterward he rode his bay back to the tie rail in front of Doc Kroll's, tied him up, and ascended the outside stairs to Kroll's office.

This time his knock was answered promptly. Kroll opened the door and stood there, keen-eyed and smiling, in contrast to his surly aspect of yesterday. "Ah, esteemed colleague! Enter my parlor. What can I do you for?"

Doc stepped inside and, noting the opened bottle of whiskey on a table, said dryly, "Tying it on pretty early, aren't you, doctor? Or are you just getting into a sunny mood for attending services?"

"Oh, sure, services," Dr. Kroll said genially. "I've successfully shied away from them for some years. What it was, I was up all night to my bloody elbows in a harrowing piece of work. Its conclusion seemed to call for a libation or two. In moderation, of course. Care to join me?"

"No, thanks," Doc said coldly. "I suppose everyone in town has got the word by now."

"That you're John Fletcher Styles? Yep. What did you expect?"

"That, I guess."

Kroll went back to the desk, poured himself another drink, lifted the glass to Doc in mild salute, and took the drink in a swallow. "Damned surprised to see you back here, doctor, all things considered. Again, anything I can do you for?"

Doc briefly explained what he needed.

"Sure. Peruvian barks for quinine? I can provide all you want." Kroll looked half sober as he spoke, slowly turning his glass between his fingers and gazing down at it. "Just how much *do* you know, Styles?"

"About what?"

"As I say, I was up most of the night. I was—Christ, man. Did you think you could do what you did and then just ride back to Rincon bold as you please?"

"Make sense," Doc said with the hint of an edge. "Do *what*?"

"You telling me you didn't know you shot young Cordwainer's arm all to hell?"

"I shot at him. I hit his arm. That's all I know."

"Little more to it than that, friend." Dr. Kroll waggled the empty glass in his hand. "Last night I was summoned to the Cordwainer mansion—big house up on the hill yonder. I had to amputate Hunt Cordwainer's arm at the shoulder. No choice. Your bullet smashed the humerus all to hell nearly to the clavicula. Messy an operation as I've ever had to perform. What do you think of that?"

Doc tipped his head down, staring at the floor. His jaws were set so tightly that they felt knotted at the hinges. "Not much," he said quietly. "What else?"

"Christ, what more do you want? Matthew Cordwainer is out for your hide. When he gets it, he will nail it to a shithouse door. He said so, straight out in front of me."

Abruptly, Kroll's face closed up almost furtively. He reached for the bottle of whiskey.

Doc said, "There's more. What is it?"

"What?"

"You cut it a mite short there, doctor. What were you about to say?"

Dr. Kroll chuckled and said, "Nothing, nothing at all," as he closed his hand around the neck of the bottle. "You must be getting old-maid humors of the head, Styles—"

Doc crossed to him and clamped his hand on Kroll's wrist. "No more," he said gently, "till you answer the question."

Kroll sighed and nodded. "All right. Let go my arm, will you? Thanks." He poured his drink and downed it. "After I finished the surgery, I went out and was climbing in my buggy when I heard old Matt Cordwainer bawling orders at Elmo Jagger—"

"Jagger? He was there?"

"Sure he was there. He and a couple of his sterling compatriots helped hold the kid down the whole time I was amputating. Anyway, there I was, not far from an open window, and I caught all of it pretty well." Kroll paused, looking almost totally sober by now. "His son—his only son—is crippled for life. The old man won't be satisfied with just drawing blood, with wearing his adversaries down gradually, as he has until now. The wind is up. He's had a whiff of real blood and is out for the kill."

Word hadn't yet gotten to the guards at the roadblock, thought Doc, or they would have opened fire on him without preamble. "All right. Get on with it."

"Old Matt told Jagger just what he wanted done. Wants Jagger to take all his men and make a raid on the folks up on the Redondo Flats. Hit each place by surprise and burn it out. The families are to be run off the flats. If anyone resists—" Kroll shrugged one bony shoulder. "That's all I got."

"He didn't say when?"

"Nary a word. But he's taking off the gloves for sure."

Tonight, then, Doc thought, with the solid conviction of

old instinct. It'll come late at night. Dark for cover and everyone asleep.

Aloud he said, "I haven't been here, Kroll. You didn't see hide nor hair of me since yesterday. Understood?"

Kroll poured his drink and gazed sourly at it, then looked up at Doc. "What'll you do about it?"

"You'll hear soon enough," Doc said tersely. "If anything goes wrong, will they suspect you?"

"If they get a notion I overheard something, like enough." Dr. Kroll sighed profoundly. "For a long time now I've been threatening to take a prolonged pack trip back up into the high peaks. Do nothing at all for a spell, unless it's a lot of trout fishing."

"A man could lose himself back of beyond for a good while."

"I expect he could. Maybe for three-four weeks." Kroll paused. "You better not have been seen coming up here by anyone close to Cordwainer or Jagger."

"I'll take that chance. Will you?"

"I already have." Kroll swallowed his drink and set the glass down. "I'll fix up those Peruvian barks for you. Then show you a back stairs out of here. You leave that way."

Before he parted from Kroll, Doc got exact directions as to what places on what streams his colleague planned to be fishing so that he could, in due time, send someone to let Kroll know if and when it would be safe for him to return to Rincon.

For Kroll, in a few short seconds, had made a decision that might irrevocably change his future. So had he himself, Doc grimly knew. He'd not meant to get embroiled beyond caring for a wounded kid. Yet, step by step, he was being pulled in deeper. Matthew Cordwainer was a vengeful man, and tempting his wrath, given the money and power he commanded, wasn't a thing to be lightly undertaken.

What else can you do? Doc thought bitterly. Let him burn these people out and drive 'em away? Maybe kill a slew of 'em? If it happens, it'll be because you drew lightning on 'em.

Somehow he had to prevent it from happening. And as he commandeered his mount at the tie rail, swung aboard, and headed out of town, he had no good idea of how he could manage it.

Elmo Jagger rode up from Rincon along the switchbacks of a smoothly graveled road to the sprawling layout of the Cordwainer Milling and Mining Company. Situated on an isolated flat in the foothills, built in the form of a Greek cross, it was perhaps the single most impressive structure in all this backwoods country, if you excepted Matthew Cordwainer's tall frame mansion with its rococo gables and cupolas, set on a slightly higher elevation a quarter mile to the south.

Jagger rode past the main plant from which boomed the deafening roar of ore-reduction machinery. He halted by the building's north wing, dismounted and tied up his horse, and was admitted to the company's office area by a liveried watchman who gave him a salute of recognition, saying, "Afternoon, Mr. Jagger."

Elmo tramped down a long green-carpeted hall past rows of gilt-inscribed doors, mildly amused by how the company's opulent headquarters contrasted to beat all hell with the adjoining activity of heavy industry, raw ore, and scruffy, sweating workmen.

He opened the last door and entered a sumptuous outer office where he was told by a male secretary to wait a moment, please. A minute later Jagger was seated in Matthew Cordwainer's inner sanctum, a high-ceilinged room with rich oak paneling and leaded windows, savoring an excellent cigar that had been offered him from the humidor on the ornate walnut desk.

Matthew Cordwainer said to him with a faint, frosty smile, "How do my stogies suit your fancy, Mr. Jagger?"

Elmo waved his hand, making an idle spiral of smoke. "Passable."

"'Passable.' The finest of imported Havanas available. Really outstanding that you find them 'passable.'"

Jagger puffed on the cigar again, giving his employer a half-lidded stare through the smoke. "You sent a message for me to come up here," he said finally, mildly. "Just for the hell of it, or do you have a reason why?"

"Why do you think?"

Lounging in the high-backed chair, Jagger crossed an ankle over his other knee and shrugged. "I dunno. I hoped it might be because you'd reconsidered."

"Reconsidered? You mean as to sending you and your men out to hit those Flats people? Hit them hard?"

"Yeah. That." Jagger inspected the tip of his cigar. "On the tag end of last night, when you gave me the order, you was pretty het up. You had some reason to be. I thought you might have cooled off enough now to circle around it, sniff it over, and do a mite more thinking on it."

"Did you?" Cordwainer leaned his elbows on the desk, steepling his fingers. They were thick, stubby fingers on large hands that looked as though they'd been broken and scarred in youthful brawls, as was likely the case. Cordwainer was a stocky man, broadly built, whose physique conceded nothing to his age, which Jagger guessed was about sixty. Rolls of muscle bulged under the shoulders of his finely tailored suit. His face was ruddy and jowly beneath a cap of dead white hair, and it was bisected by a neat white mustache. On the surface he was an ordinary businessman, at ease in his role but somehow wearing an aura of imperiousness. Jagger knew nothing of his past and cared less, and yet occasionally, curiously, he wondered what drove the man.

"And how did you reckon my rethinking might affect matters, Mr. Jagger?"

"I'd hazard you are aware that was a pretty rank order. It's pushing things way out. Some people could get killed."

Again the frosty fragment of a smile. "I wouldn't have thought that consideration would weigh heavily in your line of work, sir."

Elmo felt a brief flicker of anger, but it died as quickly. "Maybe it oughtn't to," he said indifferently, "but you go pushing too hard, you could kick up a big stink with county law, even if it is headquartered across the mountains. Maybe even with a U.S. marshal, come to that."

"Suppose you let me worry about it. I have connections in high places, Mr. Jagger. Connections you'd not believe." Cordwainer paused, eyeing him sardonically. "Anything else troubling you? Is the job too rank for you and your bravos to handle? Or is it too piddling and insignificant to be worth your notice?"

Jagger had a secure hold on his temper now.

Early this morning he'd seen Matthew Cordwainer in a virtual frenzy over the maiming of his son. He'd never before seen this controlled man in anything resembling an unsettled fury and guessed he never would again. Cordwainer now had a cold, complete control of himself once more. But his goal of wiping out the Redondo Flats settlers hadn't altered by a jot.

Jagger smiled a little. He considered tapping off cigar ash on the rug, then leaned over to flip it into the big brasswrought ashtray on Cordwainer's desk. "Nothing like that. We'll handle the business like you laid it out. I just wondered if you got to consider that it was Doc Styles shot your boy's arm up and maybe you didn't want to lay what he done on all those other folks—"

"To hell with that," Cordwainer said flatly, icily. "I've pussyfooted around with these people too long. We make the strike. Now. Tonight."

"Whatever you say."

"Anything else *you* care to say, Mr. Jagger?"

"Yeah." Elmo lounged to his feet and paced a slow circle on the thick carpet, glancing over the crystal chandelier, the luxuriously leather-padded chairs, and the incongruous Doré prints on the walls. He halted, puffing his cigar, then took it from his mouth and pointed it at Cordwainer. "You want to tell me about that regulator of yours?"

Cordwainer didn't bat an eye. "Regulator?"

"Yeah. A man who hires out in cattle wars. Fellow who does dirtier work than I ever mixed into. What he does is, he waits his chance. Watches and waits for days, maybe. Then he shoots folks from cover, knocks 'em off like clay pigeons."

Cordwainer lifted his thick hands and lightly slapped them down palm flat on his desk. "You've heard. Well, damn. What can I say? Except—what's eating you? Scruples?"

"Scruples, hell. You hired this guy behind my back. Styles told me so."

"Styles did?"

"He happened on the scene when those Redondo men were cut down. Goddamit, you listen now." Jagger strode to the desk, stabbed out his Havana in the ashtray, and leaned both fists on the desk's gleaming surface. "You hired me and my crowd to handle the business with them settlers. If you're playing some shitty little game on the side, you better come clean with me. I don't hone on being kept in the dark."

"No private game," Matthew Cordwainer said calmly. "Just coppering my bets. I was getting impatient. Thought to slowly whittle down the opposition through you and your crowd. It didn't work as well as I'd hoped. That O'Hearn fellow, in particular, was throwing a wrench in the works. Didn't figure you or any of your fellows would have the belly for raw, straight-out assassination. So . . ."

Jagger dropped back into his chair. "You're a cold-blooded son of a bitch," he said softly. "So is he. Who is he?"

"That's none of your business. None of his activities need touch you. He'll do his job; you'll do yours. As I direct you, of course."

"Will I?"

Cordwainer smiled. "I think you will. I still need you, Mr. Jagger. If your pride is injured, I apologize—and will sweeten the pot accordingly. From now on you and your men will draw double pay. How's that?"

Jagger gently tapped the fingers of one hand on his knee. Angry about Cordwainer's going behind his back, he'd been prepared to confront the mining magnate, quarrel with him, and then quit and walk out. But double the pay. Jesus. He and his bunch were already being paid far beyond anything they'd ever dreamed.

"That might be all right," he conceded. "Only it'll be triple pay for me."

"Mr. Jagger, you are already pulling down twice the pay of any of your men."

Elmo just looked at him. "Uh-huh."

Cordwainer smiled wryly, and said, "Very well," and leaned forward across the desk, extending his hand. Jagger knew Cordwainer meant to try the "hand game" with him, and he responded with a grip just as powerful.

Cordwainer broke it off. Holding the wry smile, he leaned back in his chair. "It's a bargain, then. Let's go over the plans again, shall we?"

CHAPTER ELEVEN

Losing no time, Doc skirted Cordwainer's roadblock and arrived back at O'Hearn ranch headquarters by midafternoon. He told Ana O'Hearn what Matthew Cordwainer had in mind for the Redondo Flats people. And he asked if all the able-bodied men could be assembled as soon as possible at one place. He thought that Cordwainer's designs could be checkmated, but they would have to form a plan in haste and then move quickly.

Ana didn't even question what he had in mind. She was a quick-minded woman, fast to grasp a situation and then to act accordingly. At once she gave Bernardo an order to ride swiftly to each outfit on the Flats and urge the people to converge on the O'Hearn headquarters, which was more or less centrally located, for an important meeting.

Doc boiled up some of the Peruvian barks for quinine and administered regular doses of it to Danny Mike, keeping a vigil at his bedside till early evening. By then the boy's feverish thrashings had subsided, but Doc still had no idea how well the medicine was really taking hold when Bernardo returned.

Bernardo, using only imperfect signs plus a note handwritten by Doc and signed by Ana, must have gotten his message across pretty effectively. At least he'd conveyed enough urgency so that, within the hour, heads of families and older sons, if they had them, began to arrive on horseback.

By this time Danny Mike's fever had broken. He was drowsily clear-eyed when he woke long enough to ask Doc how he was doing.

"What do you think?" Doc asked.

"Alive, I guess," Danny Mike whispered. "Weak as a sick cat, though. And my ears is ringing like church bells. Not that I ever heard a lot of them."

Doc chuckled at that. He liked the kid's quick salty humor. "That ringing sound is a side effect of taking quinine. So we know it's taken hold, and that's to the good. But you shaved it pretty fine there, boy. Bear it in mind next time you feel like bucking some tall odds."

The kid only smiled and shut his eyes. Almost at once he was settled into a deep sleep.

Ana had entered the room and was standing at Doc's chairside, listening. She said quietly, "Doctor, the men are gathered. Will you talk to them now?"

Doc rose and followed her out to the yard. The door of the main house was open, throwing a lamplit glow over the men who stood there, a little forward of their ground-hitched horses.

There were maybe twenty of them in all. They were both Anglo and Mexican, with some probable mating between the races, and their ages ranged from late middle age to boys in their teens. These were the men of Redondo Flats, fathers and sons and a couple of hired hands. Probably few or none of them were fighting men by nature. But sweeping his gaze across them, Doc sized them up as a hard-bitten lot, independent as hell, who'd fight to hold on to whatever they claimed on this hardscrabble piece of country. They'd be practical enough to listen, if grudgingly, to any proposition that seemed to warrant it.

Doc stood up in front of them, meeting their unblinking stares.

"I reckon from that paper Bernardo showed you that you all know who I am," he said. "What I—"

"What we want to know, señor," a man broke in flatly, "is what is your stake here. Can you tell us?"

He was standing a few feet ahead of the others and was plainly their spokesman. He was a lean, tight-lipped man of medium stature who looked as tough as whipcord and whose hard, straight-backed dignity showed through his worn vaquero's garb. His skin was coffee-brown, finely seamed by hard living rather than age, and he was about fifty.

"Doctor," said Ana, "this is my uncle, Juan Caldeira. He speaks for the Mexican people here. As Tomás, my husband, spoke for the Anglos."

Doc stepped forward and held out his hand. "John Fletcher Styles."

Caldeira hesitated, then grasped Doc's hand in his own calloused one. His black eyes still held a hard questioning look.

Doc explained as well as he could why he'd elected to remain and help the Redondo Flats people. To his own ears, though, his words had a sort of lame and hollow sound.

Juan Caldeira's lips drew even thinner under his neat silver-white mustache. "So. That is interesting. But how true is it?"

"All of it is as I told you."

"We have no reason to trust gringos. All in this country are against us except"—Caldeira waved a hand backward at the small crowd of men—"those who have proved themselves to be as one with us. All the trouble we have in this place has come from gringos. From *Americanos*—"

"And"—Doc kept his voice to its usual easy tenor—"if my name is known to you, no doubt it has a sour taste. But I did my best for Danny Mike O'Hearn. That ought to count for something."

"Say on, señor. What idea do you have?"

Doc glanced at the fading rose-gold banners of sunset in the west. Soon it would be completely dark. There wasn't a lot of time to lay out his plan, persuade these men, and then set things in operation. He began talking. None of what he said would win him a prize for eloquence. All that mattered was convincing them. A lot of mutterings and shufflings, *sotto voce* exchanges between the men, went on as he spoke.

Then he quit talking and waited.

A bear-big Anglo whose face was mostly hidden by a gray-shot beard moved forward to stand alongside Caldeira.

"All right, Mister Styles. That's your piece. I got a few questions. Name's Jaffrey, Len Jaffrey. I'm wedded to Juan's oldest sister. Got two 'most grown boys here." He tipped his head back toward the assembled men. "I don't aim to risk their lives on no harebrained notion. You sound damn sure them Cordwainer men is going to hit us square-on right off. Tonight, even. What makes you so knowledge-able?"

"It's more than common sense suggests," said Doc. "So far Cordwainer's played pat-a-cake with you, waging a slow war to wear you down gradually so that no great fuss will be kicked up before you give up. Now he's mad as hell. And why tonight? Because if he plans to burn you out all at once and Jagger sends his outfit to hit each of your places one at a time in broad daylight, the smoke from the first would alert your neighbors. You'd all be on your guard."

Jaffrey stuffed his hands into the deep pockets of his buffalo coat, scowling. "So? Fires can be spotted a long ways off by night. Same thing."

"Not quite. These flats of yours are generally even but broken up here and there by hills, crags, washes, cross-canyons, and so on. If someone set out to raid your outfits, he'd plan it so any sign of fire would be cut off even from a short distance."

"Couldn't he split up his men and hit different places at once?"

"He hasn't that many. Maybe a dozen or less. He'll hold 'em together for each separate raid. Hit hard and fast and get it over quick."

There was a run of mutters through the group. All looked grim, but they were listening.

Jaffrey's scowl didn't relax. "Might just be. But you ain't shown us what we can do."

"I need to know more. The lay of the country, where your places are located. We'll try to figure how they will move, then set our plans a step ahead of 'em."

Doc's glance shuttled to Juan Caldeira, who was listening intently, the weathered skin at his eye corners puckered to a squint. "Say on, señor," he said.

Doc squatted down on his haunches, smoothed a patch of ground with his palm, picked up a stick, and started to sketch in the dirt. The men sidled up around him, watching. He drew them out, asking questions. He sketched in the location of each ranch house, along with lines that defined the general layout of the land. Finally, he rocked back on his heels, satisfied.

"I believe this is how it will go, gentlemen. They'll hit here, at O'Hearn's, first of all. If nothing else, old man Cordwainer will want to be sure of wiping out this place— and me with it." Doc tapped the stick on another point of his improvised map. "Next closest place as you range along the Flats is—"

He paused, not remembering the name right off.

"Antonio Perez," said a short, wry-faced man. "It belongs to me."

"Almost surely they will go for that next. Only"—Doc swept the stick between two lines of indented dirt that marked a couple of parallel-running ridges—"they will not get any farther than here."

"I do not comprehend," Ana O'Hearn said slowly. "Just what is it you propose, doctor?"

Doc said quietly, "Nothing you'll much like," as he tossed the stick aside and rose to his feet. "We will have to abandon this place of yours."

"Abandon?"

"Clear out. Leave it. They'll take it when they come. But nobody will be here."

"*Sangre de Cristo!*" The words burst from Ana in a soft, shocked explosion. It was a strong oath to come from a woman. Even at this crucial moment, it brought a frown of disapproval from Juan Caldeira. "I will *not*—!"

Doc cut in coldly, "Listen, *por favor?* Do you prefer, then, that we make a stand here? They will ride down on us suddenly, and we will be waiting for them in the house and other buildings. They will fire on us, and we will fire back. Some will be killed. Some of theirs, yes, but some of ours, too. Do you want that?"

"*Qué? Por Dios!*"

She was staring at him, fists braced on her hips, a black blazing wrath in her eyes. Her uncle loudly cleared his throat to let her know how unseemly her behavior was, and she didn't even glance at him.

"It's like this," Doc said patiently. "We sacrifice your place to save lives. They'll come here; they'll figure we—"

"They will burn it all up!"

"That's right. Then they'll head on to hit Perez's. Only they won't get there."

Jaffrey rumbled a chuckle. He came close to smiling. "Sure not. Shortest way between here and 'Tonio's is atwixt them ridges. That's where we'll be laid up. A-waiting."

"That's where, Mr. Jaffrey." Doc watched Ana as he spoke, seeing the anger blaze unabated in her face. "We'll take them by surprise and cut them to pieces. Likely none of us will get hurt at all."

"You know that is how it will go?" Ana hissed. "*Do* you?"

"It seems most likely, that's all. No man can say for sure."

"And all this will be gone—" She swept one hand in a wide circle, the other hand still braced on her hip. "All of it on your *guess*!"

"It's a little more than that, Mrs. O'Hearn." The cutting edge in Doc's tone sharpened. "I've been through this kind of thing before. During the late war—and after. You sacrifice a position, sometimes, to win a battle. Other times you sacrifice a battle to win the war. It's all the same. Winning in the end is what matters."

CHAPTER TWELVE

A COLD WIND STROKED OFF THE PEAKS. DOC, CROUCHED ON the ridge at its highest point, shivered a little. He shifted a cramped leg, rubbing a hand along his thigh to ease the ache, and found that even in this night chill his palm was sweating.

Below him the strong glow of a nearly full moon picked out the bottom of a deep, broad pass between the two straggling ridges. Tall and rock-littered, with almost no vegetation, the ridges ran irregularly parallel to each other for about a mile, then petered off into more of the mildly humpy contours that characterized most of the so-called Flats. The bottom of the pass was strewn with jagged boulders that shone whitely under the moon, throwing out long blots of inky blackness on their shadowed sides.

The men of Redondo Flats were stationed at intervals along both ridge sides. They were deeply concealed in the shadows, and they were silent, waiting.

It felt strange to Doc, getting back into action after the years he had spent staying out of trouble. Strange even after these last thirty hours of tension and violence and threatened violence. And the raking up of old cold ashes and finding that a few embers still glowed.

Caroline.

To hell with Caroline.

He remembered the look on Ana's face at his last sight of her. It had been one of hatred. Pure hatred. And it had lodged under his hide like a wasp's barbed sting.

What the hell did she expect?

It was the best way of serving Cordwainer and Jagger and his gang a hard lesson for good and all. The gathered men had seen the solid sense of it and were willing to go along. Ana's uncle and the others had beaten down her resistance with fierce arguments about what all of them had at stake. They'd agreed in a rough man-style way that it was too bad the O'Hearn place had to go. But once this was over, they'd assured Ana, they would pitch in to rebuild whatever was destroyed, build it bigger and better than ever.

Maybe because she was used to taking a man's orders and resigned to the general lot of a Mexican woman, Ana had finally given in—but choking down a bitter fury as she'd done so. Jesus, thought Doc, she has more spirit than I've ever seen in a living soul, man or woman. It's there sure enough, but I hazard it's been beaten down all her life. True, she might be wrong in this instance. But her objection had only sharpened his respect for her.

The idea had been to evacuate the place without making it look evacuated. It must seem that the O'Hearns were merely away from home for an evening, paying a casual call on neighbors. This meant that almost everything that could have been borne away—household possessions, tools and equipment, hogs and chickens, some horses and milch cows—must be left behind. Ana was permitted to take away her most cherished belongings, an assortment of utilitarian items such as blankets and cooking utensils, and some of the domestic stock. These, along with the dog Tigre and the wounded Danny Mike, were conveyed to Antonio Perez's place, to remain there for the time being. A lighted lantern was left hanging from the O'Hearn doorpost, as though to guide the absent owners home.

Crouched a few feet from Doc, the hulking Bernardo

coughed gently. Doc glanced at him, seeing his long, coarse profile etched by the moonlight, the rifle across his knees glinting where it wasn't covered by his huge-knuckled hands.

Bernardo met Doc's glance now and grinned. It was startling to see, that massive prognathous jaw parting to reveal big square teeth. Even a little frightening. Doc grinned back and pulled a couple of short sixes from his coat pocket. He stuck one in his mouth and offered the other to Bernardo, who accepted it with a silent yawn of appreciation. In keeping with Doc's warning to the men not to light any smokes, he merely clamped it between his great jaws and resumed his vigil.

Good man, Doc thought.

All of the women, children, and other noncombatants had been instructed to remain close to their homes, to stay in hiding outside any buildings where they might be trapped if Jagger's men slipped past or around the ambush.

If, Doc thought wryly. A pretty misty qualification. How could he be sure of anything? The raiders should fire the O'Hearn buildings and then, with a confident exuberance, head for the next nearest outfit: Perez's. They should take what was by far the easiest route, between these low ridges. And be caught in a savage crossfire between men stationed on either side.

But suppose it went otherwise? Let Jagger or one of his crowd suspect something was awry, that this was a setup to lure them into a trap— No, goddamit: Surely Jagger's bunch, even a shrewd man like Jagger himself, would be so elated by one easy hit that they'd ride on to a next strike without a second thought. Might be different if one of them was familiar with the general terrain. But they were all imported hands in a strange country. . . .

Someone was shaking him by the shoulder. Doc came alert with a start. Though squatting on his haunches in an uncomfortable position, he had quietly dozed off. Maybe it was a habit of his wartime training. You slept when and where you could, no matter how briefly.

Bernardo had taken a gentle grip on his shoulder with one hand; the other pointed southward. Lifting his head now, Doc saw a ruddy glow of light fanning out above the intervening lifts of land. *That's it.* The O'Hearn house and outbuildings were afire.

In the dark he heard a few quiet murmurs from the men; then they faded away. Doc blinked his heavy-lidded eyes. He fished in his pockets to assure himself that he had cartridges to spare if he needed them. God, he was tired. But that was all right. The knowledge filed his mind to a fierce alertness.

It seemed a small eternity before a faint clink of iron on stone reached him. They were still too distant to see, cut off by ragged twists of terrain. But they were coming. The waiting men were dead silent. A few thumbed their rifles to cock; that was all.

At last the file of riders came in sight, jogging around a turn between the ridges. Moonlight lay like spilled milk on the rocky ground, picking them out as clearly as a noonday sun would. Their voices drifted. They were talking quietly, a little boisterously.

Now? No. A little longer. Just a little.

Now.

Doc's own first shot was to be the signal. He snugged the Winchester against his shoulder and settled on the foremost horseman. That should be Jagger.

He pressed the trigger with a slow, gentle care. And knew, with a marksman's instinct, just before he sent the shot off, that it was a bad one. He nicked the horse; it whickered and reared. But the rider held his seat and reined the prancing animal down.

The Redondo Flats men opened up on both sides. The whole body of raiders was strung out loosely below, and now it dissolved in a melee of shouts and shots, the screams

A SPECIAL OFFER FOR LEISURE WESTERN READERS ONLY!

Get FOUR FREE Western Novels

Travel to the Old West in all its glory
and drama—without leaving your home!

Plus, you'll save between $3.00 and $6.00
every time you buy!

GET YOUR 4 FREE BOOKS NOW— A VALUE BETWEEN $16 AND $20

Mail the Free Book Certificate Today!

FREE BOOKS CERTIFICATE!

YES! I want to subscribe to the Leisure Western Book Club. Please send my 4 FREE BOOKS. Then, each month, I'll receive the four newest Leisure Western Selections to preview FREE for 10 days. If I decide to keep them, I will pay the Special Members Only discounted price of just $3.36 each, a total of $13.44. This saves me between $3 and $6 off the bookstore price. There are no shipping, handling or other charges. There is no minimum number of books I must buy and I may cancel the program at any time. In any case, the 4 FREE BOOKS are mine to keep— at a value of between $17 and $20! Offer valid only in the USA.

Name_____

Address_____

City_____ State_____

Zip_____ Phone_____

Biggest Savings Offer!

For those of you who would like to pay us in advance by check or credit card—we've got an even bigger savings in mind. Interested? Check here. ☐

GET FOUR BOOKS TOTALLY *FREE*—A VALUE BETWEEN $16 AND $20

▲ Tear here and mail your FREE book card today! ▲

PLEASE RUSH
MY FOUR FREE
BOOKS TO ME
RIGHT AWAY!

Leisure Western Book Club
P.O. Box 6613
Edison, NJ 08818-6613

AFFIX
STAMP
HERE

of terrified or wounded horses, the racketing boom of gunfire echoing between the ridges, the ambushers keeping up a steady fire from their protective shadows, the moonlit riders returning fire confusedly, shooting blindly.

It was a brief and halfhearted stand. The bull-booming voice of Jagger yelled for them to clear out, to get out fast.

One man was knocked out of his saddle, then another. Even given the difficulty of downhill shooting, the dense vagaries of black shadow and milky moonlight, more bullets found live targets. Men were reeling in their saddles as they streamed out of the trap. Doc heard himself yelling as loudly, as exultantly, as the men around him. He gagged against the stink of cordite, and his shoulder ached from the heavy recoil of his weapon.

The shooting slackened away. A haze of pale dust hung over the trail, blending with the shredding cloud of powder smoke. It settled slowly. A pulse of ebbing hoofbeats sounded to the north; then it, too, was gone.

Doc eased stiffly to his feet, rubbing his shoulder. A taste like acid filled his mouth. He tramped slowly down the ridge side, climbing over and around rocks, and Bernardo hulked at his heels. The others, too, began to vacate their positions, descending to where men lay silent or groaning on the boulder-strewn level.

A horse was down, thrashing and neighing. Doc tramped over and ended its misery with a single shot. Juan Caldeira moved up beside him. "Five," he said quietly. "Three are dead, two are badly hurt. That is about half of them?"

"Close to," Doc said tonelessly. "Almost that."

"And others were wounded. They rode away, but we hit some of them."

"Yes."

Caldeira was eyeing him closely. "It was not a good thing for any of us. It turns us to animals. But you—of us, I would think you would take it best."

Doc said nothing.

Caldeira said, respectfully, "You are *hombre y medio*, doctor."

"A man and a half?" Doc shook his head bitterly. "I'm not even half that."

"I think so. I think you are."

CHAPTER THIRTEEN

THE FLATS MEN HAD LEFT THEIR HORSES GROUND-HITCHED some distance away, off behind one of the ridges, so that they'd give no alarm. Now they were fetched, along with a wagon that Doc had readied to contain any dead or wounded. Working by lantern light, he tended the three wounded raiders. One of them, hit in the right lung, died as Doc was tying off his wound. The other two, and the three dead ones, were loaded into the wagon, and the Flats men set out for Antonio Perez's place.

They reached it as the gray of false dawn was paling the horizon. The ranch people were gathered in the yard when they rode in. Doc looked for Ana O'Hearn, but she was nowhere about. Young Bridget was standing by, a worn *rebozo* hugged around her slim shoulders, and she came over to him.

"We seen the fire," she said in a flat, lifeless voice. "The light of it, anyways. So they burned it all up?"

"I'm afraid they did."

She eyed him with the merciless honesty of the very young. "Ma couldn't abide to watch it. I did, though. We heard all the shooting even from here. I guess you done what you had to. Even if it got our home burned up."

Doc nodded wearily. "That was the cost, Biddie. I'm

sorry. You got what I made you pay for, if it helps any. We dealt them a hard one.''

"I can tell Ma that much, then.''

"We made them pay, too. For your father and those other men they killed. If that means anything.''

Biddie said tonelessly, "I'll tell her that, too,'' and then turned, walking toward the house.

In spite of the tired letdown he felt, and with the bloody success of his own strategy still fresh and foul in his mouth, Doc conferred briefly with Juan Caldeira and Len Jaffrey. With O'Hearn gone, Jaffrey seemed the likeliest spokesman for the Anglo settlers. He and Caldeira agreed on the bare bones of procedure as Doc suggested it.

They couldn't discount the possibility of a swift and savage retaliation. Doc didn't believe there'd be any; Cordwainer and Jagger would be made cautious now. If they could be spared from other duties, a few men should ride out to patrol the flats every day and all day. They should be well armed. If they picked up any odd signs that might indicate Cordwainer and company were preparing another move, it should be reported at once to Caldeira and Jaffrey. In the meantime, the O'Hearn place should be rebuilt, but enough men should be spared from that task to continue work on the road building that would give the Flats a wagon connection with the road to Vestal.

Caldeira and Jaffrey went along with all of it but hedged a little at Doc's final suggestion. That was to break Cordwainer's roadblock between the Flats and Rincon. He felt they should do it right away, on the heels of their successful ambush.

"Man, I don't see this thing,'' Caldeira said cautiously. "Why should we do it?''

"A couple reasons,'' said Doc. "You'll want to lay up plenty of provisions against the weeks to come. Now you're starting to fight back, anything might happen. Why not copper your bets in advance? Second, I think a sudden move defying Cordwainer, following up what we did last night, is in order. That way he'll damned well know it wasn't just a passing gesture of defiance."

"But then we will go against the law. We'll have to cross Cordwainer's land, no?"

"Only this once. And we can manage it without any bloodshed. . . ."

It was an hour past full dawn when the cavalcade of Redondo Flats men came down the pine-flanked road to where the barricade of boulders was laid across. There two guards waited, grim-eyed and hunkered down behind the rocks, rifles showing.

Doc, heading up the line of riders, pulled to a halt about fifty feet from the guards. He thumbed his hat back on his head and leaned his crossed arms on his pommel. "Morning, gentlemen. I suggest you stand out of the way."

"Damned if we will," the older guard said.

"And dead if you don't. Look to either side of you. And behind you."

The two exchanged quick glances and then, more slowly and carefully, looked around them. Four men were easing out of the girdling pines and brush, one to either side of them and two at their backs. All held rifles at the ready. The guards were caught flat-footed. With all their attention diverted by the approaching horsemen, they hadn't paid a lot of heed to their flanks and rear.

"Your choice," Doc said. "Throw your artillery away. Or try to use it."

The older guard hesitated for a few seconds, then cursed once and dropped his rifle. He pulled his waist gun—with his left hand at Doc's cautioning order—and let that fall, too. The younger guard stood tense and hot-eyed. Finally, after a rough order from the older man, he discarded his weapons, too.

"Very good," Doc said. "We're bound for Rincon on

business. A couple of my friends will remain to keep an eye
on you fellows till it's concluded."

It was that easily done. A wagon containing the three
corpses and the wounded men was driven up to the
roadblock; the men were lifted down and commended to the
attention of Cordwainer's guards. A dozen husky Flats men
made quick work of rolling aside the obstructing boulders.
Doc and his contingent rode on through, along with the
vacated wagon and three other empty ones.

In Rincon they found that word of last night had already
gotten around. One sure sign was that they had no trouble
obtaining supplies. Before now, because of Cordwainer's
influence, some merchants had been reluctant to trade with
the Flats people. Doc purchased a supply of ammunition
and advised his friends to do the same. He also bought
himself some rough work clothes.

He toyed half heartedly with the notion of calling on Alex
and Caroline Drayton. If they were to be allies of a sort, any
breach should be healed. But he thought, with a bitter
anger, To hell with it. The recent encounter was still raw in
his mind.

Like it or not, though, he was up to his neck in the affairs
of the Flats people. He'd drawn Cordwainer's wrath onto
them, and he was responsible for whatever happened next.
Almost tacitly he had assumed a leadership he did not want
and which the nominal leaders, Caldeira and Jaffrey,
seemed just as tacitly to accept.

Why? Because, obviously, they respected his reputation
as a fighting man. The savage irony of it almost made him
laugh aloud. Caroline couldn't have had her wish more fully
realized if it all had come about exactly as she'd planned.

Days passed. The ranchers' defenses were shored up.
Work on the wagon road to Vestal went on under Len
Jaffrey's direction. Doc labored side by side with Bernardo
and Juan Caldeira and his three sons to clear away the ashes

and rubble and rebuild the O'Hearn place from the ground up.

Big pines were felled, cut into logs, and snaked to the site by team and go-devil. The logs were shaped and side-flattened with adze and drawknife, fitted and notched together, as the walls of the new buildings rose. The straightest and most knot-free logs were laboriously whip-sawed into planks for roofs and window frames and crude pieces of furniture. It was the meanest sort of labor. Doc took his turn with the others, standing in a pit and working one end of a cross cut saw.

At first, he found the work pure hell. His muscles ached with a bone-wrenching weariness; his hands blistered and reblistered. He sweated away pounds till he looked like a gaunt caricature of himself. At night he was barely able to eat, and afterward he'd topple exhaustedly into his blankets and a dreamless sleep. Getting up in the morning, he could hardly drag himself erect. His temper turned black and fierce, and for a time he wasn't fit to exchange the time of day with.

Still, he kept doggedly on the job, somehow keeping up with his work-toughened companions. He began to harden out. His appetite came back; so did his weight, this time in hard, spare flesh. His hands calloused. His wry humor returned, softened, less acidly bitter than it had been. Something else came, too, that made him vaguely uneasy.

Working alongside these rough, untutored men, treating their families' illnesses whenever the need arose, he was drawn more and more into the grain of their hardscrabble lives. Into their problems, their joys, their heartaches. He was starting to care about things again, becoming vulnerable as he hadn't been in years. A part of him fought bitterly against the feeling.

No more, goddam it. Who needed any more getting hurt from too much caring? That's all it ever came to in the end. . . .

Danny Mike's wound healed quickly. Pretty soon he was hobbling around on a crudely improvised crutch, wanting to help out with the work. But Doc strictly forbade it. For sleeping quarters he and the kid and Bernardo shared a tent improvised from an old tarpaulin, and it was an amiable sharing.

Once a man was used to Bernardo's looks, he generally found him easy to get along with. Doc knew from his medical studies that probably something Bernardo was born with, or that had happened to him later on, had affected his hypophysis gland—the small, oval, reddish-gray body at the base of the skull of which science knew so little—to produce his abnormal size and deformities. His control of his vocal cords had likely been impaired by a siege of scarlet fever in his youth. Doc's medical experience had also taught him that a physical malfunction no more made the man than clothes did. Yet it had isolated Bernardo as much in his way as Doc felt isolated in his. So friendship between them came easily.

With five men on the job every day, the buildings were roughly finished in a little less than three weeks. They hammered down the last boards on the new barn roof on a Saturday noon—the split-wood shakes could be fashioned and nailed into place later—and Juan Caldeira broke out a bottle of tequila and passed it around.

Doc took a generous slug when his turn came, then went into a coughing fit. His stomach felt like a nest of raw fire. Going on three weeks without a drink had dulled his easy familiarity with inexpensive liquor.

He joined the other men in their laughter, and they all tramped over to the cook fire where Ana and Biddie were taking turns at revolving a spit that held the carcass of a small pig. Crackling in its own juices as it turned over a glowing pit of coals, the roasting meat gave off a rich aroma that made the tired, hungry men groan with anticipation.

"You will have to wait," Ana told them. "It needs

another hour at least. And Tia Dolores and her daughters are not yet here.''

That made the men groan again.

This was to be a celebration. The Caldeira womenfolk were due to arrive any moment, bearing a lavish spread of other edibles. It was, in fact, to be a minor-scale fiesta. Doc, who was exceedingly fond of hotly seasoned Mexican food despite its effect on his long-ravaged stomach, was looking forward to it. Biddie was turning the spit now while Ana basted the pig with a deliciously odorous sauce.

Doc winked at Biddie. "Don't turn it so fast, mavourneen. I get tired of seeing those same teeth marks each time they come around."

"Hah!" Juan Caldeira gave his shoulder a hard nudge with the bottle. "This one was the youngest of my sty, Juanito. As tender as a suckling. Almost. Take the bottle; drink. Maybe in its depths you will find more clever thoughts to say."

Grinning, Doc accepted the bottle, tipped it high, and took another slug that went down better. He handed the tequila to Bernardo and then glanced at Ana.

Since the night when the buildings were torched, she hadn't deigned to give him a jot of attention more than bare civility demanded. If he greeted her of a morning, the only response he got was a courteous *"Buenos días"*; anything else he said was acknowledged by the briefest nod. If it was something she couldn't avoid answering aloud, she'd reply with a few impersonal words. Without being directly hostile, she'd closed him neatly out of her world. If he'd ever wondered how it might feel to be a wax dummy, he no longer needed to guess.

The more he thought about it, the more disgruntled he felt. Sure, in luring Jagger's bucko lads into a trap, he'd gotten her precious home burned up. But she and Biddie were still alive and on their own land, all the driven-off stock had been rounded up, some possessions had escaped destruction, her husband was avenged—admittedly cold comfort—and the tide seemed turned against Cordwainer. Now the house and outbuildings were restored—as good as new and better. You'd think all of that would more than balance out the account.

After another minute or so of idle banter, Doc eased away from the group and walked off toward the barn. He wanted to be alone for a spell and sort out his irritations.

Going around back of the barn, he halted. Danny Mike was standing hunched in an intense crouch, his body stiffly braced by his bent left leg. On his right side the crude crutch was socketed under his arm while he took awkward aim with a pistol at a tin can he'd set on a fence post. He cocked and pulled trigger. The hammer fell with a hollow snap.

"What," Doc said, "d'you think you're up to, Deadeye?"

The kid wheeled in surprise, almost falling on his face. He flushed. "Heh? Nothing. Thought I'd try out my leg a little more."

"And your brother's hogleg."

Danny Mike smiled, hefting his late brother's old cartridge-converted Colt .44 in his palm. "Just something to pass the time."

"Look—" Doc walked over to him and took the revolver from his hand. "If you have to do it, do it right. Here—"

Still riding his private edge of irritation, Doc spent the next fifteen minutes priming Danny Mike with a more detailed tutelage of what he'd told him scant seconds before the boy had downed the Hermosillo Kid in a Rincon saloon. By the end of that time, Doc's edge was worn off, and he was viewing his own reaction with a quiet, private disgust.

Getting het up against Ana's treatment of him was bringing him back full circle, to how Caroline had made him feel. And the hell with that. He had killed Ana's husband; Tom O'Hearn had died at his hand, no one else's. He couldn't rule that fact out of any other considerations.

By now he was eyeing Danny Mike with misgivings. The kid had picked up so quickly on everything Doc told him you'd think he had a special instinct for it.

"Thanks a heap, Doc," Danny Mike said with his easy, engaging grin. "Tomorrow I'll load up this old donkey cannon and burn a little powder on some targets. If I ever get half as good as you, it will be plenty."

"Look," Doc said slowly. "Don't get too carried away with this gun business, all right?"

Danny Mike looked at him blankly. "Why not?"

"It can land you between a rock and a hard place, that's why not," Doc said coldly. "How does your leg feel?"

"Getting better right along."

"It doesn't hurt like hell?"

"Sure it hurts some. But—"

"It takes just one second, boy. One second and one bullet. But it can end a life. Or cripple a man to the end of his days. Try bearing that in mind."

Danny Mike nodded, but with a faintly puzzled look. Doc strode back around the barn. Before he reached the front, he heard a rattle of harness, then a snuffling of team horses drawn to a halt. It must be the Caldeira womenfolk arriving. But coming around the corner of the building, he saw it wasn't. A surrey had pulled up in the yard. The Draytons were seated in it.

"Fletch!"

Alex grinned widely as he spoke, waving a hand at Doc. Then he stepped to the ground and handed Caroline down. She, too, looked in Doc's direction, but her lips wore only a small, fixed, enigmatic smile.

CHAPTER FOURTEEN

IN SPITE OF THEIR TENSE PARTING OF A FEW WEEKS AGO, DOC had no particular difficulty being agreeable to Alex and Caroline. Another encounter with them had been bound to come, and he was pretty well braced for it. By now the Redondo Flats people were aware that his being here was due to a summons from the Draytons, whom he'd vaguely described as old friends.

Alex and Caroline greeted Ana, offered their condolences, and said they were sorry about being unable to call on her before now. Ana nodded gravely and said she understood.

"But now you are here, you will join our celebration? It is for the new house."

"Thank you, Mrs. O'Hearn." Still holding her pleasant smile, Caroline shuttled a glance at Doc. "You're looking remarkably well, Fletch, I must say."

"I always did have a weakness for clean living," said Doc. "You're looking a sight better yourself, Alex."

"Feel it, too. That blasted hole in my leg finally took a notion to heal properly. So it seemed time to get back to the mining proposition. Hear you folks had quite a spot of excitement here about three weeks past. And that you had a key role in it, Fletch."

"People talk," Doc said idly, aware of Ana's curious

gaze moving from the Draytons to him and back again, as if she sensed the hidden currents there.

The Caldeira women—Juan's wife, his three daughters, and his two daughters-in-law—came riding up in a spring wagon laden with more edibles, steaming hot food stowed in earthenware vessels.

There was another round of greetings and some introductions of people who hadn't met, and then the food was ladled onto tin plates and passed around. Juan Caldeira carved generous portions of barbecued pork, and his womenfolk served it up with lots of chatter and laughing.

Squatting on his heels beside Doc as they ate, Alex rolled the hotly spiced food gingerly around in his mouth. "It's a gala occasion," he observed. "Naturally, Fletch, we were surprised to learn that you'd decided to take a hand in this game, after all."

Caroline, seated on a bench with two of the Caldeira girls, raised her gaze from her plate. "Changing one's mind, they say, is a woman's prerogative. It would seem to be a man's, too."

Doc said, "That's right," giving her a show-nothing smile that matched her own.

She looked very smart in her dove-gray riding habit with its fancily draped skirt, a tricorne hat perched on her coiffed shining hair. He felt the old, unshakable attraction, but it seemed oddly detached, as if he stood outside himself and was studying his own feelings. His anger with her had quietly dwindled, in any case.

"Caro and I thought we would ride up and have another look at the old mine works," Alex said. "Any of you fellows care to go along?"

"*Mil gracias,*" Juan Caldeira said. "My sons and I have had a fill of hard work these weeks. I think we will eat and drink more, and than we will sleep."

"How about you, Fletch?" Caroline asked. "Have you seen our mine workings yet?"

Doc shook his head.

"Then why don't you go with Alex? I would as soon remain here and chat with the ladies."

Doc felt mildly irked. He remembered that in some of Caroline's demure but quietly superior moods she'd often shown a talent for oblique mockery. He used a fragment of tortilla to scoop up the last of the sauce and *frijoles* on his plate, then laid the plate aside. Just now he could do without Caro and that damned Mona Lisa smile of hers.

"Sure. Why not?"

He and Alex climbed into the surrey, and Alex put the team in motion with a word and a touch of the whip. Doc had little to say, and Alex was in a talking way, so he just listened. Soon Alex was thoroughly immersed in his subject, Richardson's old mine and the possibilities it held. A lot of the terminology he rattled off was Greek to Doc— all about rakes and drifts, foot walls and hanging walls, stopes and crosscuts, and so on—but he'd spent enough time in mining camps to follow the gist of Alex's talk.

Anyway, now that he was heavily involved in this high-country feud, he needed more exact ideas of what exactly was at stake. Also, he was genuinely interested. He liked to hear a knowledgeable man talk about his own specialty. Lots of people thought it boresome, but Doc always figured you could get nothing better out of any man than his effusions on whatever topic he knew best.

Besides, it diverted any conversation from more personal, and possibly touchy, matters.

They climbed a switchback road that led onto a series of shallow heights, natural benches terraced out of the foothills by ages of erosion. From here they had a panoramic view of the Flats and beyond them to the north a slight lift of land obscured by distance but showing rusty red slopes patched with the dark emerald of scrubby salt pine.

Alex pulled up the team and pointed that way, to the lower left, with his whipstock. "Over there, Fletch. See those raw places and all the talus that's spilled down the slopes? And those few buildings around? Cordwainer's mine works, and they're set square up against the peaks. That's why they catch all the runoff and why Cordwainer's diggings got flooded out."

"About that," Doc said slowly. "I know we'll be working against time to get the mine operation up here under way before all the water's drained off . . . but just how much time do we have?"

Alex laughed. "Well, it's not quite as urgent as I may have made it sound before. I was really het up about the ethical aspects of it. The water level on the Flats did drop rapidly at first. Now it's slowed, but it's still dropping. It may take a year, even two years, before the inevitable happens, but it will. The land up here was hardscrabble to start with. Gradually the watershed will be depleted until cropping or herding on a scale large enough for the Flats people to make a living off it will be impossible."

"How bad will it get . . . finally?"

"No saying for sure. The whole plateau is fed by that watershed, but it won't dry up completely—just be drastically lowered. And there'll be residual sources of water, from mountain streams and seasonal rains and the like. The Redondo folks will still be able to farm and raise cattle in a marginal way, with the aid of irrigation ditches. But none of them will ever in God's world be able to make a living off the land alone once Cordwainer's mine drainage has done all its dirty work. That's why the mine operation—and what it will mean to these people—*has* to work out."

Again Alex got the team moving. After another half hour of jolting up the sharp switchbacks of the poorly rutted road, they rolled onto a lofty rise that showed a spill of the red talus from mine excavation down its long flank. Alex pulled up in front of a cluster of weather-beaten log buildings, and they descended from the surrey. He led Doc on a tour of the buildings, identifying each: a headquarters office, a commisary, a bunkhouse, and a boiler house adjoining a hoist shack.

"Everything's in pretty good shape yet," said Alex, thumping his palm against a wall log. "About as Richardson left it when he ran out of money. We'll have to do a little fixing up here and there, shore up some of the timbering in the drift tunnels. But it won't take long, and the labor's free."

"I'd like a look at this silver ore of yours."

"You'll have it, soon as we get the operation under way. Can't take you into the shaft now, because we'd need men to stoke the oiler and lower the cage hoist. But I've inspected it thoroughly a couple times. At the breast of ore down on the second level . . ."

Alex broke off with a laugh, taking out his pipe and tobacco pouch. "I get too carried away. Scratch a mining man and you find a damn bore. We're not dealing with a monumental fortune here. Just a moderately good strike. One big enough to ensure all of us who are in on it with a comfortable, if low-grade, prosperity. Which brings us back to my proposal of your cut of—"

"Forget about that," Doc said curtly.

Alex eyed him a measuring moment, then shrugged. "Whatever suits you. So far, in any case, you seem to have sunk a deep stake of your own here. For whatever reasons."

"Don't ask me why, Alex. Things happen, that's all."

Alex nodded, gazing down at his pipe as he packed it with tobacco. "It's none of our business, I guess. Mine or Caro's. Naturally we couldn't help wondering about your change of heart. Apparently you got pulled into it by helping young Danny Mike."

"Call it that."

Alex smiled as he struck a match on the log and puffed his pipe alight. "Not to be specific, then—why is it that we cynics who profess disbelief in humanity become the most impossible altruists under the sun? You and I were always cynics of the first water. Remember those talks we used to have—Lord, way back before the war?"

"We weren't much more than kids then. People change."

"Have we? Sure, we may get fed up around the edges. We may even stop caring for a while. But we usually come back full circle. Look at me. Look at you."

"Mmm." Doc took a short six from his pocket and lit it off the fading flame of the match Alex held out. "They say every cynic is a destroyed idealist. Only he's not. He tries to be. Tells himself he's shed all his damn-fool ideals. That's when he gets to passing judgment on other people."

"Right." Alex nodded. "And after that he gets feeling guilty because he's aware that he's not all that damned perfect, either."

"Yeah." Doc frowned at the tip of his cigar as he drew on it deeply, coaxing it to a live coal. "He's expected too much of other people. And himself. Hell of a note."

Alex left out a soft, explosive laugh. "Damn it, Fletch, it's good to talk like this again. The way we used to."

Doc smiled crookedly. "Half-assed sophomoric philosophizing, you mean?"

"Sure. But a man doesn't outgrow that, either."

"I reckon he doesn't."

Doc held out his hand, and Alex grasped it. Something that had died out between them long ago was kindled again. Not really that simple, Doc thought. Nothing ever was. But why beat the real answer to death?

As they walked back to the surrey, Alex said, "Why I really came up here today was to check on the road the Flats people are building from here to meet the one between Rincon and Vestal."

Doc told him that the road was coming along; Len Jaffrey was in charge of the building crew, and they had it close to completion.

"That's good to hear." Alex winced a little, holding his game leg awkwardly stiff as he climbed up to the surrey seat. "The real reason for the road, as far as I'm concerned, is to provide a connection with the ore-reduction mills at Vestal . . . since the ones in and around Rincon are all controlled by Cordwainer and other local muckamucks."

Swinging up beside him, Doc said, "Caldeira told me it was you who first proposed the road and laid out the route. But that's a hell of a long way to transport a lot of heavy ore."

"It is." Alex shook the team into motion. "Did Caldeira tell you that we intend to build a mill of our own close to the mine?"

Doc nodded. "And that you mean to sink more mine shafts as the operation develops. I'd had the idea from what you told me before that a lot of the work was already completed. All the money you said that Caroline and you had invested—"

"All of it's committed to the project, yes. Until we get some solid work under way, we've left it to accumulate heavy interest in various capital investments. Some of them are pretty wildcatty for nice conservative folks like us"— Alex grinned a little—"but we figure the stakes are worth it. Anyway, that's what we're gambling our future on, Caro and I. And what we plan to pour the bulk of our money into—the mill and the new diggings. But first we want to get Richardson's old mine back in operation. So I laid out the new road to run down as straight from here as possible."

They cut across the heights on a southwesterly course over the partly graded road. Doc himself hadn't seen what had been accomplished on it since the day of his arrival at Rincon, and he'd seen nothing at all of what had been done on this end. It was a fair "country job" of road building, he thought, a nice steady descent off the benches. But Alex wasn't wholly pleased. The heavily weighted ore wagons would have to negotiate almost impossibly steep slopes, he pointed out; if a brake lever snapped, you'd have a runaway wagon and a potential disaster for driver and mules alike.

There should be switchbacks on the worst slopes so that the wagons could snake down them more easily.

The country became more heavily forested as they descended from the heights, and soon they picked up sounds of team-drawn scrapers and men's strident, yelling voices hoorawing the animals. A week ago Len Jaffrey had told Doc that all the tree-felling to clear the road had been completed and most of the stumps and rocks had been grubbed out. The big job that remained was to get the thoroughfare evenly graded for wagon traffic.

Alex guided the surrey over a last humpy turn in the road. Below them, maybe a hundred yards away, was a tableau of sweating, cursing men and straining horses operating the scrapers, driving them in crisscross fashion across the roadbed to level and build it up.

Bossing the job was big Len Jaffrey, bawling out orders in his bull voice. Now he glanced up toward the surrey, one hand shading his eyes against the sun. He gave Doc and Alex a wave of recognition, flashing a grin out of his gray-shot ruff of beard.

At almost the same moment came a fusillade of shots.

Gunfire erupted in a pale shroud of powder smoke high on the hill flank south of the road workers. Doc saw one man spin under the impact of a bullet and plunge onto his face.

In an instant the scene was in chaos as men dashed for trees or deadfalls or boulders, for anything that might serve as cover. Some of them had weapons laid by and were scrambling for these.

Alex pulled up the surrey, his hands frozen on the reins. Doc, the man of action, sprang from the seat and ran down the incline, silently cursing himself for not being armed. He hadn't thought to bring rifle or pistol on a simple jaunt to see the mine works.

Another of the Flats men was cut down before he reached

shelter. The man hit the ground without uttering a sound, bright crimson spraying from his shattered head.

The shootist on the slope turned his attention to Doc now, pumping at least four shots at him. Two of the slugs kicked up dirt close to his running feet.

Too damned close! Swearing bitterly, Doc dived for the ground and hit it rolling sideways. He let his impetus carry him on, still rolling, to the edge of the roadway. A fifth shot sent a fan of dirt stinging against his face. Then he lunged onto his hands and knees and scrambled behind a jumble of rocks and stumps and was cut off from view.

By now all the men below were laid up in cover. Those who had rifles were returning fire, directing it blindly toward the powder smoke that marked the rifleman's position.

The assassin fired twice more, deliberately and calculatedly. But not at the men. Two of the scraper-hitched mules collapsed in their harness, kicking away their lives.

As abruptly as he'd begun, he ceased fire.

Doc thought with a bleak conviction: Nobody hit him. Time any of us gets up there, he'll be clean gone.

The men of the road crew kept up a perfunctory fire at the same spot for a couple minutes more, and then the shooting dwindled off.

Doc eased slowly to his feet and into the open. No more gunshots came. Wearily, he tramped down to where the road workers were laid up. They, too, were coming out of cover, the run of their dazed mutterings punctuated by savage oaths.

Two men had been shot stone dead. Another man was sitting on the ground, grimacing as he tugged off a boot to examine his blood-soaked leg. He'd been struck in the calf, a slight flesh wound.

Doc had lost sight of Len Jaffrey. Looking around for him now, he found Jaffrey on his knees by a dark-skinned youth of sixteen or so. The boy was twisting on the ground, gripping his upper leg, his teeth clenched against soft squeaks of pain.

Jaffrey lifted his stunned gaze to Doc. "My boy Tim," he said. "I think his leg is clean busted."

Doc knelt down, too. With his clasp knife he ripped away the soaked fabric of the boy's trousers. The thigh was a mess. A little probing by Doc's sensitive fingers told him that the femur was shattered to fragments just above the knee.

"Smashed all to hell," he told Jaffrey in a low, savage voice. "Goddam it! I told you to keep a couple of men on watch wherever there's a high place. Anyplace where that son of a bitch could get a clear shot at you or your men—"

"I done it!" Jaffrey said vehemently. "I done it like youu told me! I put Ernie Compton and Fred Wills up on that slope with guns! Jesus, I don't know what . . ."

His voice trailed off, and his gaze turned hard, locking Doc's. "My boy's leg," he said almost gently. "How bad is it?"

Doc straightened up. He swung a glance at Alex, who was coming up to them now at a limping trot, and then at the roadworkers as they spread out and started up the long wooded slope, moving warily, their guns ready.

They wouldn't find a damned thing. But he should, Doc supposed wearily, get up there and inspect the spot for himself before the damned fools trampled out any useful sign.

"Damn it, Styles!" Jaffrey roared. "Timmy's leg! What about it?"

Doc's glance shifted back to him. "It'll have to come off," he said flatly.

CHAPTER FIFTEEN

DOC WENT UP THE SLOPE AND YELLED AT THE ROAD workers who were already beating the brush to knock off and stay where they were. Then he began his own search of the terrain, crouching and weaving through trees and rocks as he studied the ground.

It was the same as before. The assassin had ghosted away from the place where he'd been in ambush, leaving no sign at all. Again Doc found a scatter of spent cartridges. From his pocket he took the shell case he'd recovered from the previous site of ambush and compared it to a recently fired one. They might have been ejected from the same repeating rifle, but that particular model of Winchester was as common as grass.

It was the same fellow, though. Had to be. Patient and deadly and watchful, he must have awaited his chance these many days. Once the guards' vigilance had begun to relax, he'd made his move.

Compton and Wills had been posted well apart on the high ridge. The killer had stolen up on each man in silence. Compton's skull was crushed. A single blow of a rock, a club, a rifle butt—whatever was used—had laid him out. Wills was unconscious but alive. Not even a fracture, but his scalp would need stitching.

Later. Just now Doc's main concern was young Tim Jaffrey.

"It can't be, Doc," Len Jaffrey said huskily. "Jesus, you can't just— Ain't there no other way?"

Doc told him in unmistakable terms just what would happen if the leg wasn't amputated. It would end in agonizing and drawn-out death, the worst imaginable for a human being, short of cancer. Doc described to the last detail how it would go and then told Jaffrey to make up his own mind.

"He's your son," he said.

They took young Tim to the nearest ranch headquarters, the O'Hearns', in the surrey. At first, the jolting motion of the vehicle made him scream with pain. Soon, mercifully, he passed out. Doc had a man ride ahead to tell Ana O'Hearn what had happened and what preparations to make.

When they reached the O'Hearn place, she had everything ready. The big trestle table had been scrubbed clean to the grain with strong soap and boiling water; a kettle of water stood steaming and ready on the hearth. Doc's surgical instruments had been boiled and laid out on a snowy strip of cloth. Anticipating their use, he'd sent back to Taskerville for his medical equipment and a supply of drugs, and the twice-a-week stage that ran between there and Rincon had delivered them a few days before.

Doc primed young Jaffrey with opiates. Even so the boy was semiconscious, mumbling and twisting on the table, as Doc gave everyone their instructions before commencing surgery. The powerful Bernardo stood at the head of the table, ready to hammerlock Timmy's neck and shoulders when Doc gave the order. Against Doc's advice, Len Jaffrey and his other son, Aaron, had insisted on helping, too.

"It's the nastiest business you're ever likely to see," Doc warned. "There's others can restrain him."

Jaffrey said only, "You wasting time, Doc. Get to it," as he and Aaron took up positions on either side, Aaron next to Timmy's sound leg and his father alongside the smashed one.

Doc hooked his spectacles over his ears and glanced at Ana by his side. Her lips were set, and her skin looked tight drawn over the bones of her face in the sallow flicker of the lamp that Biddie, standing on the other side of the table, held to light the scene. Ana did not look at him as he told her exactly what to do. When he would have repeated his instructions, she said impatiently, "I know—I know. Go on."

Doc jammed a roll of linen against the boy's leg to help control bleeding in the major blood vessels. Then he snapped, "Tourniquet!"

Ana handed him a rope of twisted cloth. Doc secured it above the linen wad, making it as fast as he could.

"Hold down," he told the men. "Scalpel—"

The three clamped their hands on Timmy's trunk and legs. Doc made the first cut, drawing the incision in a rough pattern on the lower thigh to form two long flaps of muscle that would serve as a pad between skin and bone stump.

Timmy Jaffrey's screams filled the room with such an excruciating din that Doc almost had to shout his next orders. As blood welled from the fleshy trough, Ana soaked it up with fresh linen and clamped forceps and linen pads on the severed vessels at the places Doc indicated with a motion of one finger. In a brief side glance he saw that her face was as calm as a bronze madonna's. Even though he'd expect just such aplomb of her, it was plain her rough life had left her no stranger to the ways of primitive surgery.

Already in a thick narcosis, Timmy now subsided into near unconsciousness except for a spastic twitch now and then as Doc looped whipcord sutures above the forceps and then continued cutting. Muscle fibers parted neatly under the blade as he worked upward from the first incision.

Having exposed the femoral artery, he directed Ana where to apply clamps. He severed the artery with a single stroke and sutured, then treated the bluish vein in the same way.

"Will you raise the leg, Mr. Jaffrey? Straight out, if you please."

Doc made another cut at the rear of the lifted leg; the last major bleeders were clamped and sutured. All the fleshy tissues and blood vessels were now secured against hemorrhaging.

The toughest part was to come. It would take just an instant to accomplish, but it would have the closest savor of hell any man was likely to taste in this life.

Doc lightly tapped a slim white column adjoining the thigh bone. The leg muscles jerked frenziedly, as if with a life of their own. "That," he said quietly, "contains the nerves. You boys brace down like hell when I give you the word. Put all you've got into it."

The pool of light picked out the faces around the table. All were glistening with sweat. The room was close enough for sure but not that warm. Doc was aware of the runneling wet blotches on his own shirt, back and front.

All right.

Even as he lifted the knife, blinking a little dazedly against his own nervous strain, he jerked at a touch on his forehead. It was Ana, patting away sweat with a fold of linen.

Doc worked his finger under the nerve and set the blade. "*Now, men!*"

One quick slash.

Young Jaffrey's whole body surged upward in a spasm of agony. His screaming seemed to fill the little *sala* endlessly before finally trailing off. His body went limp.

At Doc's word, Ana handed him the bone saw. He pushed the muscles up as far as he could above the level of incision and laid the tempered steel blade against the thigh bone.

The saw glanced and bounced for a rough instant, then grooved firmly. Bone dust sifted down from the marrow-red femur. In less than a minute it was done.

The leg came free, rolling sideways in Len Jaffrey's hands. He looked at it, his bearded jaw working.

"Set it on the table," Doc said mildly.

The rest of the job, suturing the flaps and bandaging, was a precise, unthinking chore. Doc finished up neatly and swiftly, then wiped his hands on the last shred of clean linen when Ana silently handed it to him.

He went outside to clean up at the wash bench. The afternoon shadows were stretching late, and around him was a low-pitched murmur of voices, fluid Spanish and gruff Anglo. When he'd scrubbed away the blood and sweat and straightened up, drying himself on a frayed towel, he found them gathered around him.

Some gave him a word of thanks or blessing; others simply gripped his hand. Caroline and Alex were the first to say their good-byes, Caro not neglecting to show him that Mona Lisa tilt of her lips on parting, and one by one the Flats people took their leave.

Doc and Bernardo and Danny Mike dug hungrily but silently into the meal Ana and Biddie dished up. Afterward Doc went to the back room to check on Timmy, who would convalesce at the O'Hearn ranch. The boy was in fever, his sleep restless. He was still deep in opiates, and Doc meant to keep him that way through another day.

When he returned to the *sala*, Bernardo and Danny Mike had left for the cabin they shared with him; Ana and her daughter were clearing up the supper dishes.

Doc went to the open door and set his shoulder against the jamb. He took out one of his few remaining short sixes—he hadn't located any of his own noxious brand in Rincon—and thumbnailed a match alight.

Some of the men had been for organizing an immediate retaliatory attack on Cordwainer's holdings and serving him

some of his own medicine: taking lives for lives taken. Doc
had put his foot down flatly on the notion. A pitched battle
wasn't the answer. Heavy blood had been drawn on both
sides already. If they wanted it that way, they'd do it without
him.

"Getting pretty damn pussyfooted, ain't you, Styles, for
the sort they say you been?"

Without acrimony, Doc had eyed the speaker, a grief-
stricken man whose only son had been cut down. "That's
right," he'd agreed mildly.

One battle, won or lost, wasn't the war. And Doc had his
own notions on how to conduct it. He'd voiced them briefly,
and most of the men had muttered agreement. But today's
toll had been a costly one, and Doc knew he would not
attend tomorrow's mass funeral or listen to women's muffled
sobbings. . . .

He felt Ana move up quietly beside him. Gazing out at
the night, neither of them said anything. Doc took a step
outside, thinking to depart the *sala* without a word. Instead,
he turned to face her, feeling awkward as a boy.

"Would you like to walk out a little?"

Ana nodded. She got her *rebozo* and adjusted it around
her shoulders before they stepped out into the warm night.

They didn't walk far, just making a slow circle of the yard
and staying inside the dim pool of light from the windows
and doorway. As Doc cudgeled his brain for something to
say, it was Ana who spoke first.

"You and the señora—Mrs. Drayton—have known each
other from before."

It was a statement, not a question. And it wasn't
necessary for her to add, *And you were close*. The
suggestion was already in her voice, her faintly smiling
glance.

"A long time back, yes," Doc said shortly.

And nothing has changed. She didn't have to say that
aloud, either. He took off the spectacles he'd forgotten to

remove and tucked them in his shirt pocket, saying sourly just to have something to say, "Hate these blasted things."

"But it's not so easy to go without them if you must shoot a man."

Doc felt a coldness lock in his chest. He had killed this woman's husband. She couldn't know that. Yet . . . there was a small needling in her tone.

Keeping his voice even and deliberate, he said, "Doesn't matter in my case. I'm near sighted. You pull out a gun and point it like a finger and shoot. If the target's a way off, far enough to be clear, say, a few yards—"

"Then you kill him. I see."

Doc came to a halt, and so did she. They faced each other in a cold silence that stretched way out.

At last he said, "I have never killed a man who was not standing straight up in front of me and had every chance. And there were only three of them in more years than your daughter has lived."

"Then why do you have *muy mal* reputation?"

"Things get around. Men talk. In lonely places, around fires, in saloons and bunkhouses. It's a hard country, Mrs. O'Hearn, and a lonely one. You needn't be told that. Men without women, without families, maybe without futures, maybe with nothing in their bellies but whiskey, talk. A lot is made out of nothing. I have a knack with a gun, that's all. It's been done up out of proportion."

"Why?"

"I've been in a lot of scrapes," Doc said grimly. "I'm a magnet for trouble, or maybe I've looked for it. I can't always tell which. But I've shot up quite a few men and never taken a scratch on my own carcass—since the war. That's luck. People like to make magic of it."

"But quite a few men, you say—"

"A man doesn't die of a gunshot wound that easily. He dies just as fast or slow of a scratch that takes blood poisoning. I've seen men get shot through the head or the heart—believe it or don't—and live. The human animal is a mighty tough critter to kill. Sometimes."

"You say it so very well, doctor. But I know it is the truth. I have seen such things."

Ana began to walk again, slowly, and Doc fell in beside her. Without looking right at her, he was aware of her fine animal grace. She gave out an incredibly earthy aura, this woman, a sensuous something bred of the soil, of the sun and wind and turning seasons. of living close to a fertile earth.

She said idly, thoughtfully, "I have seen a man fall when a bullet hit his head. But it only bounced, and then he got up again."

A little startled, Doc almost chuckled. But he kept his face still and said, "Yes, the skull is very hard bone. Fancy that. If a man swings on another, barefisted, he's more likely to break his hand than hurt the other guy." He held up one hand, fingers spread. "Look at your hand sometime. Study it. It's an amazingly intricate assemblage of joints and small bones. Actually fragile."

Ana reached out and took his hand and held it next to her own, nodding gently, entirely unselfconscious. "I see it is so. Yes. Think of such a thing."

She let go his hand and moved on. Doc swallowed hard as he kept apace. Her touch had gone through him like an electric shock. Jesus. Was he crazy or what?

Their circuit of the yard was taking them past the open door again, and he glanced at her in the spill of stronger light. Madonna—was that the word after all? Danny Mike had told him she and Bernardo were half Apache, half Spanish-Yaqui. Leastways Danny Mike thought so; he wasn't rightly sure of the mixture. There was something proudly primitive and defiant in her fine carriage, the strong bones of her face. Something smoky and soft, too, in the lamplight. She must have been scarcely older than Biddie when she'd wed. There was not a trace of gray in her jet-

black hair, and tonight she had let it down, loosely framing
her face, and this, too, gave a limning of youth and
softness.

Ana stopped again, and now her look was troubled. "I
should not have been as I have been to you. It was wrong.
You have been right, and for our good. But the old place—
burning it all of a night."

"I understand."

"*Comprende?*" Her black-stone eyes looked past him.
"Do you?"

"Yes. All that you knew was here."

"All," she whispered. "Of a sudden Tomás was gone.
Then . . . the house. It was our home. All our life was
here. I bore our three children under that roof. Two died
under it. It—" She shook her head from side to side,
slowly, her gaze fixing his face. "I was wrong. I liked you
when we met. Then suddenly I hated you."

"Now?"

"It is late. *Buenas noches,* doctor."

"Fletch. My friends call me that."

"I have noticed." A smile as enigmatic as Caroline's
touched her mouth. "Good night."

Doc walked to the cabin where Danny Mike and
Bernardo were already snoring lightly in their bunks. He
undressed in the dark and slid under the blankets, the straw
tick crackling sharply. He lay quietly, not at all tired, his
thoughts churning sluggishly.

Finally, his mind drifted.

Ana stood beside him. The cabin was deserted but for
them, and she was in lamplight, her flesh golden as her
fingers moved and her clothes fell away. Her lips moved
soundlessly. There is a need. Always there is a need. He
choked on the pounding of his blood, his eyes burning at the
sight of her clean and woman-muscled body, gold smooth,
curved and hollowed, two conical breasts tipping high and
brown-nippled, and the triangular black mat of maturity

where a flat belly joined the leanly rounded thighs. In a quick motion she descended beside him, nestling and molding and compliant. Then the smiling lips changed; they mocked him, and the face wasn't Ana's anymore.

It was Caroline's.

Doc jolted awake, coming up on his elbows. Sweat crawled on his face, and he scrubbed a shaking hand across it. He nearly swore aloud. But there was only darkness and the snoring of his companions. He eased back and let his tense flesh relax, his hard-beating heart slow to normal. But there wasn't much sleep for him that night.

CHAPTER SIXTEEN

THREE MORNINGS LATER DOC WAS YANKED FROM A DEEP and comfortable night's sleep by a rattle of gunfire. He swore and groped for the Navy Colt under his lumpy pillow. Then he swung his feet to the floor, hobbled to the small east window, and peered out.

Danny Mike was standing near the tack shed with his brother's pistol. He was punching empty shells from the weapon, and now he reloaded it and settled it in the holster at his hip. He crouched, hands spread, then pivoted quickly on his near-healed leg, drawing and firing. Pale chips flew from a chunk of firewood set off a ways from the shed.

The grouping was damned good for the distance. Those old Colt .44s bucked like a son of a bitch when it came to accuracy at any distance. Danny Mike had absorbed Doc's advice as a sponge soaks up water.

And Doc warmly regretted that he'd ever given it.

Swearing sleepily, he pulled on his clothes and went outside to join Bernardo, who was bent over the wash bench, bare from the waist up, splashing water on his head and torso, spluttering like a winded walrus.

"Hey!" Doc called. "You, Danny . . . come here!"

Obediently, Danny Mike sheathed his gun and trotted over. Doc wondered if he only fancied that the boy's smile held a twist of braggadocio, almost the hint of a sneer, as he said cheerily, "Morning, fellows. What's up?"

"Your head," Doc said flatly.

"What?"

"Get it out of the clouds. I want you to look square at something. See that?"

He pointed at Bernardo's back where the brown skin on the left side showed a dark scar the size of a marble. Doc said, "You know what did it?"

Danny Mike nodded. "A bullet. Long time back Bernie got shot in a hunting accident."

"Uh-huh. That's where it went in. You want to turn around, Bernardo?"

The giant had been eyeing them quizzically, and now he turned from the bench and faced them. Doc pointed at a fist-size swell, a blackened ugly scar, on the same side in front.

"Out," Doc said coldly. "Taking with it pieces of tissue and nerve and hide, a whole section of rib, and, by a damned lucky stroke, no vital organ."

Danny Mike flushed. "I seen it before," he said almost sullenly.

"No. You took notice was all. You never saw it. First time you handled a hogleg, you shot a man dead. You got damn lucky, splitting his heart in half the first shot. He got lucky, too. A few inches lower—I've seen gut-shot men die for days. Die in fever and convulsions. Death? I've heard 'em beg for it. Scream for it."

"Damn it, Doc, ain't you ever heard of shooting as a sport? I was just fooling around with this thing—"

"Horseshit, sport. Killing—that's all it's good for. Killing and nothing else.. You got it in your head now you downed one man and figure that makes you Young Wild West himself. In your head, every time you pull trigger, you see a man."

"An enemy!" Danny Mike said hotly. "We got plenty

and to spare, haven't we? You saying you wouldn't shoot to save your life?"

"No," Doc said gently. "But I can hope I'll never again be forced to. Any decent man can hope that."

Danny Mike's face was scarlet. He pivoted on his heel and tramped up to the house.

Bernardo grunted a few words in his own odd patois, which, by now, Doc had learned to follow. "That's right," Doc said with a wry smile. "When you haven't lived very long, you have a lot to learn. Come on, let's go up to breakfast."

There wasn't much talk as they ate. Ana and Biddie, as they set food on the table and then joined the men, noted the quiet tension, too, and had little to say.

Afterward they split up for the day's work. Danny Mike and Bernardo returned to an unfinished chore of applying blab boards to some spring calves in order to wean them. Doc's business was what it had been for three days now, and his destination lay away from the O'Hearn headquarters.

"Fletch—"

Ana's low voice halted him as he was about to follow Bernardo and Danny Mike out of the *sala*. He paused in the doorway. "Yes?"

"I know what you think," she said quietly. "Danny Mike. With the gun. You think he has a bad streak, *no*? But he was not like this before."

"Before he killed a man."

"Maybe. But I have thought maybe it was getting wounded in the head. Could it do something to how he thinks? I have heard of such things. But *quién sabe*? Here I talk, and you are the doctor."

Doc rubbed his chin. "Could be something to it, Ana. I didn't know him before, remember."

"What is to be done?"

"Wait. Watch him." Doc shrugged. "The brain's a

delicate thing to fool with. Any lesion might heal by itself.
Just wait and watch."

Ana nodded, eyes somber with a darkness of worry. She
hesitated as if about to say more but only nodded again and
went back to clearing the table.

Five minutes later Doc was in the saddle, heading south
and west. He brooded. Too damned much lay unspoken
between Ana and him. Caroline had not lost her edge in his
thoughts, but Ana grew stronger in them day by day. Trying
to fight the feeling only seemed to intensify it.

No damned good. He had killed her man. She need never
know. But he would know. To stay near Ana and live with
that knowledge? Or—if he came out and told her? No good,
either.

Why in hell had he stayed on? Savagely and bitterly, he
knew he should have cleared out as soon as he'd delivered
the wounded Danny Mike home. No damned involvement.
Now it was too late. He hadn't merely sunk a stake; he had
sunk all his being here. For the first time in John Fletcher
Styles's life, he felt like a man who belonged. . . .

Riding steadily, Doc cut the road leading from Richardson's mine inside an hour. He followed it down off the long
heights almost to where the work detail was camped and
then left the road, swerving up a pine-clad slope to his left.

After the assassin's last strike, Doc had warned the road
builders to tighten their guard. Their sentries should be
rotated every couple of hours so that lethargy and boredom
wouldn't cause anyone's attention to slack off again.

Meantime, Doc had his own ace in the hole. For three
days he had laid up on a pinnacle of rock that terminated the
west end of the ridge paralleling the road. It gave a wide
overview of the roadway for nearly a mile, except where a
few shelving juts of granite or clumps of big pine cut his
line of sight.

Today, as he did early each morning, Doc quit the road
well before he reached the camp. He rode slowly up an

ancient game trail that snaked through the trees, always alert, rifle resting across his pommel.

No way of telling where or how the regulator might hide himself. He had infinite cunning, infinite patience. He was a professional right to his heels. He left no track, no betraying sign of how he came and went unseen. Doc was sure of just one thing.

The assassin knew him.

A few days ago, when he and Alex had come suddenly on the scene, the rifleman had promptly turned his fire on Doc, who had been running hard and made no easy mark. Yet the killer had swung from more stationary targets to direct all his shots at Doc until he had dived for cover.

Who? For hours Doc had culled his memory with no success. Nothing distinguished this fellow's methods. Doc's trail had sometimes twisted across that of hardcases who hired out as regulators in cattle wars. He could tick off a dozen names in his head and not settle on any one for sure.

Doc was the guiding force here; the assassin knew that, and he'd once known Doc well enough to pick him out instantly and from a distance.

Mulling it over, Doc rode on and upward on the pine-shrouded trail till he was high above the camp. Now he cut away from the path and pushed on through a hundred yards of trees and brush till he reached the bottom of the crumbling pinnacle. He dismounted and tied the bay to a sapling, slipped its bit and loosened the cinch, then circled to the back of the steep granite spire. Slowly he scaled it, digging his boots hard at rotted talus. It was a short climb, and he made it one-handed, his left hand gripping his rifle and a haversack containing grub and water.

At the top he hunkered down in a ring of boulders that would absorb and reflect a fierce heat against his body as the sun climbed. It was a miserable stand, and he had endured it for three days.

But today should be the last one.

Len Jaffrey's crew had long since finished clearing the entire roadway from one end to the other. Today, it looked like, they should complete the job of scraping it to a rough level that would give both light rigs and heavy ore wagons a direct access to the road leading to Vestal. The Flats people would no longer be dependent on Rincon or its merchants and services. All the high-handed power that Matthew Cordwainer commanded in and around Rincon could no longer touch them.

Not in a legal way. But Cordwainer had already taken off the gloves. Elmo Jagger and the regulator had shown that. The real fight, Doc knew, had only begun.

He watched the work go on down below, the faint shouts of teamsters hoorawing their animals drifting up to him. Doc's line of vision lay between two slabs of rock where he could crouch and see most of what went on without being seen. The crew was aware that he was on watch up here, and he hoped the knowledge would stiffen them against the tense dread they must be living with after the last assault.

The other sentries were scattered about halfway down on the ridge flank. The regulator would have to work down above and behind them to get inside clean rifle range. If he came at all, he would be more cautious than ever. Any final strike at the road crew must come today, for by tonight the job would surely be done.

Though he could survey a vast section of the ridge from here, Doc knew his position would be of little use in spotting the regulator's approach. The man's woodcraft was uncanny. And the dense pine growth cloaked the whole ridge enough almost to hide the movements of a small army.

Doc gambled on spotting the powder smoke that would mark the assassin's first shot, then scrambling down off the spire as fast as he could and heading on a beeline to cut the regulator off. If the man were really hungry to draw blood— and some of these kill-crazy bastards were, despite all their

caution—he might run a calculated risk and infiltrate the
sentries just to get a few potshots at the road crew.

But would he look for a man at his back, far above him
and far to his left? Doc hoped not. That's why he'd
deliberately avoided the camp in his comings and goings
from this lookout. If the assassin had spied on the camp
these last days, a good set of field glasses would tell him
that Doc wasn't in its vicinity. Any chance to nail the son of
a bitch hinged on his not being aware of Doc's presence till
Doc was almost on him.

The sun mounted. Doc grew sleepy as the day wore
toward noon. He had to fight for alertness. The dazzling
heat turned the cordon of rocks into a furnace. He'd escaped
this ordeal just once, on the second day's watch, when the
sun was banked over by gray clouds. Today would be a bad
one. He was grateful for the cushion of pine boughs he'd
fashioned; it let him crouch for hours without getting too
cramped, and it protected his butt from the scorching rock.

It was maybe a quarter of noon when Doc, casting an idle
glance off to his right, caught a sun wink of light. Just a
fleeting flash from a height of rock among the trees a few
hundred yards away. So bright and sudden it could only be
made by a glance of sun on glass or burnished steel.

Binoculars. Or a gun barrel. The binoculars, Doc thought
promptly. The regulator would have the sense to dull or
stain the metal parts of his rifle.

In an instant Doc was clambering down the pinnacle on
the side opposite where he'd seen the flash. He made a soft
noise of "Ho-shuh," a calming word, to his horse, which
had been raised by Navajos. The animal pricked its ears and
stood rock-still. Just a horse's whicker from this direction
would warn the assassin.

The heavy undergrowth that lent the regulator cover now
served Doc as he stalked the stalker. He moved in quick
silence, every sense on a hair trigger, reckoning by instinct
when and where his path would intersect his opponent's.

Mote-swimming shafts of sun slanted through the pine boughs. Jays and squirrels chattered lightly at his passage. An alert ear might make something of that, but it couldn't be helped. The killer would be wary, but mostly of what lay ahead of him.

Easy, Doc counseled himself. You have the edge. He won't be looking for you.

His line of advance took him down the ridge at a slight angle. Ahead of him the trees were thinning away, and he moved more stealthily than ever, rifle up and ready. Suddenly he saw a man's shape stir darkly in the forest gloom, limned by a mottled stream of sunrays, the shape dropping to one knee now and bringing the rifle to its shoulder.

Doc knew what he was aiming at. One of the sentries was laid up just ahead. The killer didn't intend a strike at the road crew itself. He'd settle for knocking off as many of the guards as he could.

Doc was a little behind the regulator, far to his left side. The dim light was a handicap, but Doc's line of aim was clear. No obstructing brush. He butted the Winchester to his shoulder and, just before he tightened an eye along the sights, thumbed the hammer gently to cock.

The slight noise didn't alert the regulator. He was drawing a bead, taking his time. And Doc squeezed the trigger.

The regulator dropped. But the way he went down told Doc it was mostly a reflex of plunging to the ground to make himself as tight a target as possible.

Echoes of Doc's shot were still trailing off when the killer fired from the ground. Bark flew from a tree about two feet to Doc's right. But he was already behind another tree, aiming again, levering and triggering, pulling off a shot a second.

The killer scrambled to his feet, a dark running figure as he crashed away into the brush and was gone. Doc left cover and ran after him.

Moments later he hauled up, swearing savagely. The bastard had done it again. His trail had faded on the carpet of pine needles. No use trying to track him. Even if he could manage it, the fellow would gain ground on him all the while. And up ahead, at any place of his choosing, he could lay an ambush.

But Doc knew something else. He had hit the man. Wounded him hard.

A spray of ruby drops marked the place where the regulator had gone down. And in his retreat he had stumbled and fallen again, leaving a great splash of blood on the rusty pine needles. A trail of blood drops went for another fifty feet and then ended suddenly. Somehow, in his flight, the assassin had managed to stanch the blood flow. After that Doc found nothing.

By now the man was far gone. But badly wounded. How badly?

Already, somehow, Doc had a black intuition about the answer to that question.

CHAPTER SEVENTEEN

ONCE MORE ELMO JAGGER SAT IN THE SUMPTUOUS OFFICE where he and Matthew Cordwainer had last faced each other. For the last time, Jagger had thought back then.

It had been a bitter meeting. Cordwainer had been seething because of Jagger's failure to burn out and run off the Flats rabble and to kill Doc Styles. Elmo, on his side, had been in a contained but dangerous fury caused by the killing and crippling of his men that had wiped out nearly half his crew in one stroke. In the exchange of hot recriminations, after Cordwainer had called him a stupid goddam bungler, Jagger had declared that he and his men were through. He'd demanded all pay owed them to date. Cordwainer had scribbled out a time slip, and Jagger had taken it to Cordwainer's bookkeeper, who paid him in greenbacks. Within the hour he and his men were riding south from Rincon.

But more than a month later, a message from Cordwainer had reached Jagger at San Tomás, a mud-hut village near Tucson, Arizona. Brought by a special messenger, the letter was brief, to the point, and yet almost cryptic. But there was no mistaking the offer it made. The figure, a round, flat-named sum tailed by a lot of zeros and no decimal points, had stood out in stark print on the fancy letterhead paper.

A man would have had to be pluperfect crazy to turn
down anything like that amount of money. And for a single
job.

"Understand," Cordwainer said now in a clipped,
toneless way, "you don't collect a cent until the work is
done. And to my satisfaction."

Jagger exhaled the fragrant smoke of his Havana and
smiled through its haze. "Well, that shines all right. I don't
reckon you trust my abilities a whole lot anymore, huh?"

"Have I reason to?"

Jagger stirred his head in honest negation. "I got to hand
it to Styles. He outthought and outfought me, the fox-eyed
bastard." His tone held a note of pure admiration. "I felt
pretty raw about my boys that bought it that night. But that's
the game in our business. Man deals in it to win or
lose . . . all the way."

"You'll take my word, then."

"Hell, no," Elmo said almost cheerfully. He leaned
forward and carefully tapped ash into the desk tray. "Job's
done, you'll pay inside the hour. Right to the damned cent.
Or things will happen. Like, you know, that's a fine big
house you got on the hill. Must have taken a sight of money
and labor and time to build."

A wintry smile brushed Cordwainer's lips. "It took most
of a year to build and furnish. The furnishings had to be
freighted hundreds of miles. And it could all burn up in a
couple of hours. Any day, any night, anytime. I can't post
guards forever. Think of that."

"You will," Elmo murmured. "You'll think about it.
That's why I don't need to trust your word. Or," he added
arrogantly, "any man's. What is it you want us to do?"

Jagger bent his head, gazing at his crossed boots, gently
drumming his blunt fingers on his chair arm as he listened to
Cordwainer lay it out. When the mining mogul had
finished, Jagger raised his head, cuffed his hat back with a
big fist, and nodded slowly.

"That'll be some job. Dynamite is touchy stuff to fool
with less'n a man knows what he's doing."

"My man's an old hand. He'll set the charges. You and
your men take care of the rest."

"All the rough stuff, you mean."

"That's *your* specialty. So I once heard tell," Cordwainer
said acridly. "If you can manage not to foul the nest this
time around, I'll be grateful."

"You'd dámn well better be." Jagger spoke almost
absently, massaging his jaw with his right thumb. "Coming
in, we stopped at the Shortbough to wet a whistle. Heard a
few scraps of talk."

"Did you?"

"Yeah. What I gathered of it, that regulator of yours had
a run-in with Styles and came off half best. What's
happened to your man? He out of commission now?"

"That's none of your business."

Elmo showed his big yellow teeth, grinning. "Public talk
is any man's currency. Caught himself some lead, I hear."

"Then perhaps you heard he made it clean away,"
Cordwainer said coldly.

"Uh-huh. I just wonder in what shape. Seems he got
fetched the same message I did." Elmo uncrossed his boots
and rose, still grinning. "That Styles, he may look a
lightweight. But he fights in the same weight class old John
L. did. Purely heavy, huh? Makes it interesting."

"No doubt. I'll see you later, my boy."

"That you will, pappy. You surely will."

Doc had an eerie sensation of falling as the car descended
into the vertical blackness of the mine shaft. He instinctively wanted to seize hold of something to brace himself, to
put a false sense of solidity under his feet. But Alex stood
on the platform beside him, teetering carelessly on his heels
and idly puffing at his pipe. So Doc stood quietly rigid,
hands fisted in his pockets, listening to the hiss of cables

above, the clinking of guide irons that formed an enclosing cage for the car. They passed the first level and halted at the second one.

Alex, holding a lighted candle in a spike holder, stepped from the platform and led the way down a horizontal drift tunnel that branched off the main shaft. Doc hated the place. It felt claustrophobic. He hated its dank smell, the trickles of seeping water that laced the rocky walls, the soggy clump of their boots through puddles. He hated the dismal dark and the wavering flicker of candlelight that threw ragged shadows and made oily shimmers on the water.

The track on which the ore cars operated ran down the center of the gallery. Once, Doc and Alex stepped aside as a couple of men, one of them Bernardo, pushed a loaded car past them toward the cage, exchanging nods with them. The grind of wheels on track filled Doc's head with rumbling echoes.

God. He was glad this was only a brief visit below ground to satisfy his curiosity. How could men work out their lives in holes like this even if it were the price of survival?

Alex talked cheerfully as they moved on, twice halting to jab his candle spike into a timber so he could examine places where the cribbing and timbering had been newly reinforced, pointing these out to Doc, rattling off a lot of technical crap that slid off Doc's hearing like water off goose feathers.

Finally, they came to a cavernous room hollowed out of the wall. Alex called it "a stoping of the pocket." Half a dozen of the Flats men, their candles spiked in the fresh timbering, were laboring with sledges and single jacks, drilling out chunks of ore. The din of racket in this confined place was terrible. Dim as the candlelight was, it picked out thousands of facets of glittering silver, and even Doc, with his untrained eye, was impressed.

"What do you think?" Alex asked.

"That you're really on to something here."

"*We* are, you mean, Fletch. If you—"

"As I said before, go to hell. Which this comes fairly close to, both in proximity and atmosphere."

Alex chuckled. "Don't like it down here, eh? Most of the fellows don't. Some can't stand it at all. Juan Caldeira, that tough old bird, quit and went home. But two of his boys took to the work fine. These men aren't miners by trade or inclination. But they're not working for wages. It's a cooperative venture, and full of promise. For the future. For them and theirs."

Alex gestured toward the darkness of the tunnel beyond. "Down that way's the old working head that Richardson abandoned. Want to see it?"

"No. Let's get out of here."

They headed back along the track.

"Only equipment we have is what Richardson left behind," Alex said, "and it's pretty bum stuff. Must have been third hand when he bought it. But I've sent out for new equipment and more of it. Ore cars, track, mules, tools, all we'll need to get the operation running full steam."

"It's your money. How far you figure to stretch it?"

"To the limit. And beyond—why not? You've seen the breast of the ore. Just what we get out over the next few weeks will serve as collateral for financing; for a rapid branching out, for a development of this whole range. Hell, Fletch—this is the stake of a lifetime, and the sky's the limit! I look forward to when we'll set up our own ore-reduction mills right here on the Flats. . . ."

There was a flush and shine and fever to Alex's excitement. He believed in the rightness of his cause, and he was a mining man clear to his toes. It softened the edges of what otherwise might be naked greed. In Alex Drayton, desire for wealth wasn't the consuming lust that it was with Matthew Cordwainer. Alex's ambition was tolerable, if grandiose, and once more Doc felt pleasure that their old friendship was renewed.

As they reached the main shaft, the hoist car rumbled to a stop in its descent. They waited till the empty ore car was rolled onto the track, then stepped onto the platform and were borne up to the shaft house. It was a large building a couple of stories high, laced with huge beams from which swung the tackle that raised and lowered the car. At floor level, where the shaft was collared off, a track ran out of the building to where the ore would be sorted and graded and sacked prior to shipping. Now it was just being dumped there in a great heap.

Doc and Alex walked past the sweating stoker at the hoist engine, past the big furnace that furnished its steam power, and out into a welcome blaze of sunlight. After the darkness of the mine, it hit their eyes with a dazzling force. For a moment they failed to see the man standing off left of them and the other men beyond him.

Then the leader moved forward, sun winking on his leveled pistol, saying, "Sight easier'n I figured. And we netted us a bonus, looks like."

Doc blinked at the dark form and came to a stop, careful not to move his hands. He knew the voice first. Jagger's. Now his gaze shifted past the big man to the others fanned out around the shaft-house entrance, closing in with their guns out and ready. One of them was leading a mule with a box roped to its back.

Doc had posted a pair of guards. What had happened to them?

Jagger answered the unspoken question as he tramped over to Doc and lifted his Navy Colt from its shoulder holster, then rammed it in his own belt. "Took your men by surprise. But didn't expect to find you here, Doc. Maybe Drayton, but not you. You're our bonus. So now we got two prime pigeons in hand. And the mine, too."

A couple of Jagger's men had moved past them to cover

the stoker, a stocky Flats man named Jourgenson, with their
rifles. He stopped feeding wood chunks into the furnace and
watched them.

"All right," Alex said quietly. "You have the mine.
What can you do with it? Steal it? Carry it away with you?"

"Nothing o' the sort." Jagger was chewing on a twig; he
spoke idly around it. "But I can blow it to hell and gone.
All the guys working inside it, too."

Alex's shocked gaze whipped to the wooden crate
strapped to the pack mule. "Jesus," he whispered. "You
wouldn't— My God, even Cordwainer wouldn't—!"

"*He* would," Jagger corrected him. "I wouldn't. Not
that I ain't tempted after how the good doctor set up that
deadfall for my boys. But that was part of the game."

At his order a couple of the men unroped the well-trussed
box and carried it into the shafthouse. As they went past,
Doc glanced at the stenciling on the crate's top: *DANGER—
HIGH EXPLOSIVES—THIS SIDE UP*. One of the two men warned
the other to set it down carefully.

Jagger said around the twig, "That's Sobie Shamrock.
Best dynamite man in the Territory. Works for Cordwainer."

"Sweet Jesus," Alex said faintly. "If you have any
decency at all, get our men out of there first."

"Sure," Jagger said amiably. "Killing a passel of men
that way ain't in the game. Leastways not in mine. Ain't
they just lucky." He jerked a nod at his men. "Willy, Ranse,
Lobo, Clarence. You boys go down and fetch 'em up." He
glanced at Alex. "Where are they?"

"Gallery . . . off second level."

Jagger nodded at Jourgenson. "Stoke it up, my man, and
get that engine working."

The car rumbled down the shaft with the four men. Two
of them were armed with sawed-off Greeners, and Doc only
hoped that none of them below would be fool enough to
buck a scattergun.

Alex's jaw worked. Some of the blood had drained out of

his face. "There's . . . no possible way I could persuade you not to go ahead with this?"

Jagger tipped his brows in a mild shrug. "Not any I know of. What you have in mind, hard-rock man?"

"Wealth. More than you'll see in a lifetime. It's down there. A fortune waiting to be taken out. There's a piece of it for you."

Elmo shifted the twig from one corner of his lips to the other. "There's a thought," he murmured. "But it don't go, assayer. I give my hire to a man, it's as good as my bond. My hire is to Matt Cordwainer."

"Then you're a damned fool as well as a jackleg crook!"

"Alex," Doc said coldly, not looking at him, just watching Jagger. "Quit it. Let it go."

Jagger laughed silently. "Doc, leastways you got a hatful of smarts. Might keep you both alive a little longer."

"You have orders regarding us, I take it?" Doc asked.

"You and Drayton? Uh-huh. You're the big burrs in old Matt's britches, you two. You, Doc, you're the Flats folks' fightin' arm. The assayer here is their workin' arm. What's a body when it gets both arms chopped off? Just a bucket of nothing."

"Let me understand this," Alex said between clenched teeth. "You have a game of your own complete with 'rules.' Burying all those men alive is outside the pale, yet your rules are elastic enough to accommodate the killing of two other men in cold blood."

Jagger spat out the twig. "That's about it," he said comfortably. "That's just how it is."

CHAPTER EIGHTEEN

THE TAKEOVER IN THE MINE GALLERY CAME OFF WITHOUT a hitch. The work crew was brought up in relays, four of them to each relay, with two of Jagger's men holding guns on them. The other two gang members stayed below with the remaining captives until, after three trips down and back, the Flats men stood assembled outside the shaft house.

They were twelve to six, but Jagger's men held all the artillery. And the latter were a crowd of hardcases if Doc had ever seen any. Three he recognized as members of Jagger's previous bunch; the rest were new hands. In their violent business, men came and they went, footloose or just dead.

"All right, Sobie," said Jagger. "Now it's your game down there. Need any help?"

"Could use a couple men." The dynamiter was a rawboned man in a dirty cotton singlet and a battered plug hat, and his jaw never ceased working on a chaw of plug cut. "Got to drill holes, set the charges, get 'em capped and fused. Then I got to fire 'em up in a hurry and clear out. Do it a sight faster with a couple men."

"Lobo, you and Clarence go down with him. What he tells you to do, you do."

The crate of dynamite was lifted onto the platform, along

with sledges and single jacks from the toolshed. Once more
the car began its descent, clanking and rumbling out of
sight.

Jagger looked over the sullen group of Flats men. "I
don't reckon we require having you gentlemen look on. You
can go home."

Len Jaffrey rubbed a grimy palm over his face. "Damned
if I will," he said flatly. "You aim to blow up our mine,
you're going to have plenty of witnesses."

"Now who needs witnesses?" Jagger asked pleasantly.
"My boys will escort you right to your doors. Where are
your horses?"

Jaffrey wheeled suddenly, grabbing at a guard's gun. But
the man moved faster, taking a quick step backward, then
smashing his rifle butt into Jaffrey's face. He went down
like a poleaxed steer.

In almost the same moment Bernardo seized the guard,
wrested the rifle from him, and flung him away. A snarl
broke the giant's lantern-jawed face as he rushed a second
hired gun, whirling the rifle around his head.

The man flinched back, at the same time thumbing back
his gun hammer. His rifle thundered just as Bernardo's
mighty swing caught him in the skull. Bernardo grunted and
stumbled backward, red dying his shirt. Another gang
member fired point-blank. Bernardo swayed and dropped
like a felled tree, his blood pouring out on a gray rubble of
mine tailings. He twitched once and was still.

"Hold it!" Jagger roared.

His men stood tautly ready as a surge of movement
rippled off among the Flats men. Jagger tramped over to his
fallen man, bent and tipped his crushed hat sideways, and
grimaced.

"Busted his head like an eggshell." He glanced at
Bernardo's sprawled form. "Reckon that squares it. All
right, this one." He nodded toward the unconscious Jaffrey.
"Sling him across his horse and take him home. After you

get these men to their ranches, go to town and wait for us. Won't take long to finish up here."

Jagger's bunch had left their horses hidden nearby. One of them fetched four of the animals. Another went to liberate the two mine guards who'd been captured and left tied up back in the brush; he brought them to join the other prisoners. Afterward three of the gang members mounted up and followed the mine crew, two of them carrying Jaffrey, to their horses. The animals were hobbled out on the grassy green of a cedar grove a little distance away. Doc, Alex, and Jourgenson left with Jagger and one of his men, watched the riders head double file down the long road from the mine, the three guns bringing up the rear.

Jagger settled one hip against the boulder and idly waved his pistol at Doc and Alex. "You fellows might as well relax. Take a spell to set them charges."

"What are you waiting for?" said Alex. "If you mean to kill us, why not have it done with?"

"It's like this, assayer. For what I got in mind, them charges have to be set first. When they go off, you'll be down there with the doctor and this stoker." He nodded at the bodies of Bernardo and his own man. "Them, too."

"Ah. You'll simply throw us all down the shaft. Is that it?" Alex said.

"That's it."

"And no *corpus delicti*, eh?"

Jagger looked amused. "Be harder'n hell to dig any out from under a few thousand ton of rock. Less'n some enterprising jackass wants to excavate this hole again. Only I don't 'low there'd be enough left of you boys to identify."

"That won't get you or your curly wolves off the hook, Elmo," said Doc. "Our friends will be alive to testify."

"Uh-huh. They might raise a sight of stink, too. But who cares? County law's way across the mountains. Hell, the sheriff's office is right in the hip pocket of big muckamucks like Cordwainer. So's the governor and the territorial legislature. What are you, any of you? A cardsharp and gun tipper, a busted-flush assayer, this here stoking man, and that dead dummy yonder. All of you together ain't worth fussing a feather over."

The talk ended. All of it was said. The stillness slid into a slow broil of midday heat and a drone of flies settling on the blood-patched bodies. All four men were motionless as statues, just watching one another, Jagger easing his weight against the boulder, arms folded. He didn't object when Alex let out a soft groan and settled to the ground, stretching his game leg out in front of him.

Doc stood hipshot, thumbs hooked in his belt, hat brim tilted to shade his eyes. His legs were aching, too, more from tension than anything else, but he wanted to stay on his feet. He'd been in tight jackpots before this. If anything at all broke in their favor, if the least chance presented itself, he wanted to be set for it.

Jagger's man, the one called Ranse, never stirred a muscle. His eyes were coldly pale in the shadow of his hat. He held his gun loosely trained on Doc and Alex, hardly batting an eye as he watched them.

They were all sweating profusely in the naked heat. Especially Jagger. Sweat blotched his shirtfront and armpits. He grunted something, took off his hat, and dragged a sleeve across his perspiring face. Then he clamped his hat back on, pushed away from the rock, and headed toward the shade of the shaft house. His path took him less than a yard past the sprawled body of Bernardo. What happened next was so swift, so unexpected, that Doc was caught as much off guard as anyone.

Bernardo rolled to his feet like a great cat and sprang at Jagger's back. One huge arm circled Jagger's neck from behind, whirling him around to shield Bernardo from Ranse's gun.

Jagger grabbed for his own pistol, but with his free hand Bernardo wrenched it from its holster, at the same time yanking Doc's Navy Colt from Jagger's belt and letting it fall. Jagger clamped his hand around Bernardo's forearm and tugged. A large and powerful man, he was dwarfed beside the giant Mexican. While Bernardo held him as easily as a child, Jagger's face turned darkly red, veins squirming in his temples. Then Jagger ceased to struggle, for Bernardo had cocked the pistol. And placed the muzzle to Jagger's head at the base of his skull.

Ranse had swung his gun on the two at once. His chilly eyes were wary, gauging the odds. Even if he could put a bullet in Bernardo without hitting his boss, Jagger might still die. And Ranse had to keep part of his attention on Doc.

Bernardo said something gutturally.

"He says," said Doc, "to throw your gun away or he'll pull trigger."

Jagger managed to choke out, "Ranse . . . don't . . . it's a stand off."

"Like hell it is," Doc said with calm arrogance. "I wonder, Elmo. Have you filed the sear on that hogleg of yours? If so, one wrong twitch by you and it could go off. Bernardo just might get your chum, too. Anyway, it's a dead cinch Ranse can't get more than one of us before the other two are on him." He paused. "That *is* a hair-trigger gun, Elmo, isn't it?"

Jagger said through gritted teeth, his lips peeled back, "All . . . right. Throw . . . your piece . . . away, Ranse."

Ranse hesitated. Bernardo tightened his crushing hold.

"You bonehead bastard," Jagger wheezed. "*Do it!*"

Ranse swore quietly and pitched the gun into the rubble almost at Doc's feet. Doc scooped it up and walked over to retrieve his own Navy Colt. "We're fine now," he said. "Ease off, Bernardo."

The giant released Jagger, who slipped to the ground,

coughing, holding his livid throat. Alex scrambled to his feet. "Fletch, the—!"

A grating rumble rose from the mine shaft. The car was returning. Doc said softly, "Bernárdo, watch them," and tramped into the shaft house. Ducking out of sight behind the machinery, he watched the car glide up to floor level and stop. The explosives expert and his two helpers stepped off. They halted as their gazes registered the tableau outside. In the same instant, Doc stepped out into view, covering them from behind.

"Get rid of those guns. Pull them left-handed and drop them."

Lobo and Clarence obeyed. Doc motioned them out of the shaft house ahead of him.

Alex moved swiftly to meet them, seizing Sobie Shamrock by the arm. He hustled him back inside and grabbed up one of the fallen guns.

Doc said, "What the hell are you doing?"

"I'm going down," said Alex. "Jourgenson, get the engine working."

Doc took a step toward him. "Jesus! Are you crazy?"

"Stand where you are, Fletch." A deadly and terrible intensity filled Alex's voice. "I'm going down there. I'm going to snuff those fuses. He'll show me where every charge is set. You—get on the platform."

The dynamiter's face went pasty under its mask of sweaty grime. "You're loony as a bedbug, mister. Them fuses is trimmed to time fine as fuzz. So's the charges will all go off near at once. We got less'n—"

Alex gave him a savage prod with the gun muzzle, forcing him into the car. "Start it down, Jourgenson!"

"No, Alex . . ."

Doc shaped the words as a bare whisper. It was useless to say anything. Alex, in the grip of a resolute frenzy, would hear nothing. And would be stopped by nothing. Short of a bullet.

Doc could drop a man quickly and easily at this distance. But to inflict a slight wound would require a careful aim. And a longer fraction of time. Alex seemed to read his thought.

"Don't, Fletch. Don't try it. I'll shoot you first. Dead, if I have to. Don't force it, Fletch."

The idealist and his dream. God help him. Doc stood helplessly by as the car sank into the shaft. Then he looked at Bernardo. The whole side of the giant's shirt was drenched in blood, and so were his trousers. He must have bled out plenty, lying motionless on the ground, awaiting his chance. He held a massive splayed hand tight over his side, but he was firmly on his feet, holding a steady gun on Ranse.

Doc's glance shifted to Jagger, who was sitting upright, still rubbing his bruised throat. Now Doc pulled Ranse's gun from his belt and tossed it into the rubble between Jagger's legs.

"Pick it up. Get on your feet."

Jagger closed a fist on the gun, got his legs under him, and carefully stood up. His broad mouth smiled. "A fight, Styles? An even break?"

"No," Doc said tonelessly. "An execution."

"But you're giving me a chance. Like to take it with my own gun, though."

"That hair-trigger piece?" Doc shook his head contemptuously. "You're a fool. All right, Bernardo, take that gun from him and hand him his."

Now Jagger's own weapon lay in his palm. His smile widened. He did exactly what Doc had sensed he would. Facing a gunman of Doc's reputation, knowing Doc's first shot would not miss, Jagger placed his bet on pure speed and luck. Lightning-fast, he slapped the hammer with his left hand, fanning off his shots in a blur of gun roar.

Doc had never learned the trick. He took a perceptible moment to aim and then squeeze off his shot.

Jagger had gotten off three wild shots when Doc's bullet slammed him back, staggering. He tried to steady his gun, and Doc shot him again. Jagger fired a fourth time, but the bullet drove into the rubble at his feet. Then he fell to his knees and pitched slowly onto his face.

The rattle of pebbles as Jagger fell was drowned by the explosion. The earth quaked like a living thing under the men's feet, making them fight for balance. The other explosions, trailing by moments, were only gigantic echoes of the first. And finally there was stillness. . . .

CHAPTER NINETEEN

CAROLINE STOOD BY THE SMALL WINDOW THAT FRONTED the cabin, looking out on Rincon far below. Absently, she fingered one of the frayed muslin curtains, then sighed deeply and turned to face the room, thrusting a damp handkerchief into the waist of her skirt.

Seated in a chair, hat laid on the table at his elbow, Doc said gently, "All right?"

"Am I composed? I believe so. Thank you, Fletch. You've had—" She paused, as if fumbling for the proper words. "You have had a long, hard ride. May I offer you a cup of coffee? Something stronger?"

"Coffee will be fine."

Her composure was only a glaze. It would be good for her to move about, do something, any little task that would occupy her attention. He watched her prepare the coffee, filling a pot with water, spooning in Triple X, and stooping to hang the pot from a trammel hook in the fireplace. A kettle bubbled there; stew, it smelled like, that she'd just finished putting together when he'd arrived.

After tending Bernardo's wound and getting him back to the O'Hearn place, Doc had set out at once for Rincon to tell Caroline Drayton that her husband was buried under tons of rock. In his years as a practicing physician, he had delivered similar news to more than one sudden widow. A man learned to steel himself. Or try. But this was the worst time of all. The dead man was Alex. The widow was Caroline.

After the telling, he had stayed silent, ready to leave if she wanted him to, yet somehow knowing she wouldn't. When the first shock of stunned disbelief had ebbed and she'd broken down in sobs, she had come blindly into his arms, and he had given what comfort he could, talking quietly until the storm of weeping passed.

Now she was dry-eyed and outwardly composed, her face pale and still, the reservoir of grief locked back for the time. She was like Ana O'Hearn, a woman with iron in her spirit, as much iron as nature could abide in a single person. People like that did not break. Anguish might bow and bend them; it never broke them.

She sat down at the table across from him. "I have never cried like that, Fletch. Never, I mean, that I let any other person see. Not since I was a little girl." A small embarrassment tinged her voice. "What else can I say?"

"You needn't have said even that, Caro. But thank you for saying it."

She reached for his hand on the table, pressed it quickly and withdrew it. "Do you know what he said to me once? It was just before we were wed. That . . . marrying him might prove to be the greatest mistake of my life."

"He smiled when he said it—if I know Alex."

"Oh, yes. He smiled. You know the wryly humorous way he had of putting things, especially when they cut near the bone. It would be a mistake, he said, because he was a flaming idealist and a man of action in one. A dangerous combination. A girl who wed a chap like that was buying into trouble. Because such men have a habit of being short-lived."

Doc said tightly, "He was right, too," then shook his head. "I didn't mean that harshly, Caro."

"I know. Because you are one yourself."

"Was."

"Are."

"All right. Maybe. But not like him, Caro. What he did—going down in that mine in a last-ditch attempt to douse those fuses—" Doc shook his head slowly. "It took the guts of a tiger to do that. Or the whim of a crazy man. But Alex wasn't that."

"No," Caroline said quietly. "Not crazy. But he had a reckless streak that nobody—except perhaps you and me— ever suspected. The quiet, scholarly engineer! Yet there was more to the situation than that, Fletch."

"What more?"

"We have money to develop the mine, all our savings, judiciously invested, as Alex told you. But not so much that we weren't going to be riding an awfully fine edge financially in order to make the venture succeed. And of course it *was* still a gamble, despite Alex's invincible enthusiasm—backed up, of course, by the solid results of his assay work." She bowed her head, biting her underlip. "That was his ultimate reason to make the final, biggest gamble of all. To prevent those charges from going off in the face of all odds. The mine being blown up might easily have been the final straw that would tip the balance against us."

"And reduce you to destitution."

"Utterly and completely. Behind his cheerful demeanor, Alex was living with that knowledge. It did not harrow him on his own account, understand. It was—" Again, sudden tears shone in her eyes. "It was *me*, my future and my comfort, that occupied all his thoughts. And that's what drove him to go down into that death trap!"

"You can't be sure of that. Don't get thinking that way, Caro, or it will poison the rest of your life."

"That is already done, I should think." Abruptly, she rose and walked back to the window. "But there needn't be two of you coming to such an end, Fletch." Her voice was low and hard and bitter. "Not, at least, on my account."

Doc watched her in puzzled silence, waiting for her to say more. Finally, she turned her head enough to meet his gaze directly. "Do you know how many men have died since this fight between Matthew Cordwainer and the Redondo Flats people began? Do you, Fletch?"

Doc frowned. "You mean can I give you a head count?"

"Can you?"

"Right offhand, I suppose—"

"Comparatively speaking, then. You've been in wars, Fletch; over land, water rights, mining claims. Even over slavery. How does this one compare to any of them, for its size, in the toll of lives taken?"

Doc lifted his shoulders and let them fall, wearily. "About as bad as any, I reckon."

"I thought so. And it can be stopped. I can stop it. And I will."

For a fleeting moment he was baffled. Then he caught her meaning. "The money that would have developed the project," he said slowly. "Yours and Alex's. It's all yours now. You can spend it as you please. Or not spend it."

"And I will not." Her back was stiff and straight. "Alex sparked this war, however unwittingly, when he found a fresh lode of silver in the old mine."

Doc said sharply, "That's nonsense, Caro. Cordwainer's damned greed set it off."

"Say it did. Everything else fed into it. Even my well-meant letter urging you to help. And more men died for it!"

"Sometimes," he said roughly, "a man has to fight. Has to risk being killed, even. Because the alternative is worse."

"What's the alternative—being defeated? Can't a man swallow a defeat now and then?"

"In this world," Doc said grimly, "he'd damned well better learn to. No, Caro. What he can't swallow is living on his knees. I'd die before I'd do that. So would Alex. So would any man worth his salt. And these Redondo folks are worth that and a sight more."

She eyed him for a long, wondering moment. "You meant that. You've become one of them, Fletch."

"I have. It goes deeper than any passel of flighty boyhood idealisms. I do not hone to take any man's life, Caro. Not even Cordwainer's." He paused deliberately. "There's other ways of killing. Yours, for instance."

"*Mine!*"

"You'll kill a dream. Alex's dream. And all the dying that went before will be for nothing. The Redondo people will be back where they started, but with even less."

"It's no good, Fletch." Her voice was cold and brittle. "You're asking me to give you and your friends a *carte blanche* for more bloodshed. And that I will not do."

"Alex had already sent out an order for new mine equipment. Will you let that stand?"

"I will not. I'll cancel it. Without financial backing for their project, the Flats people will have no reason to make a fight. That will end it."

"End what?" Doc got to his feet and picked up his hat, crushing the crown in his fist. "End their troubles? Not after damn near all the water on the Flats has been drained off. It'll be worst for all those families who've lost menfolk. Who—or what—will provide for them?"

"A good question. Think beyond it, Fletch. Who'll provide for the future widows and orphans your way is bound to create? Even if you win your—your damned war." Her eyes burned bright jade with tears; her lips quavered. "How much do you think all the wealth in the world will profit a woman who's lost everything that's dear to her? Go on, Fletch, back to your wars. You'll find others, I'm sure, if you outlive this one. Other things to fight over. Part of being a crusader, isn't it?"

Her words sank like claws, but oddly Doc felt no pain,

only a weary sadness. As if, once more, he had come to the
end of something and found, this time, that it was really
over.

As he turned toward the door, she said very quietly,
"Fletch, I'm sorry. That was cruel."

"Cruel or not—" He made a vague gesture with his hat.
Let it go at that. "What will you do now, Caro? Where will
you go?"

"To Virginia. Back to my people."

They were my people once, he thought. Another time
. . . another life. Aloud he said formally that he would
call on her before she departed. Then he took his leave.

It was well after dark when Doc rode in to the O'Hearn
headquarters. The dog raised a mighty barking, and the
house door was edged open, throwing a shaft of light across
the yard.

"*Quién es?*" Ana called.

Doc replied. He was stupid with weariness as he climbed
out of the saddle. His legs nearly caved under him, and he
held to the saddle for a moment, resting his forehead against
the warm leather, feeling utterly spent in body and mind.

Then Ana was beside him, and so was Danny Mike. The
boy said, "I'll put up your horse, Doc," and led the animal
toward the corral while Ana and Doc headed for the house.
His steps dragged, and he silently cursed his exhaustion,
grateful for Ana's touch, her hand on his arm, even if it
rested there lightly.

She told him to sit and did not ask questions as she heated
up cold beefsteak and biscuits and *frijoles* over the fireplace
coals. He was grateful for her silence, too, but knew she
would have to hear everything soon, or most of it. So, as he
ate his supper, he talked. She sat at the trestle table beside
him, her fine hands clasped on its top, and listened. Danny
Mike returned from tending the horse, and he leaned against
the wall, arms folded, and listened, too.

When Doc had finished, Danny Mike said, "So? What now? Do we sink another mine shaft?"

"Not," Doc said dryly, "unless you know where a mighty lot of money can be had for the asking. Mrs. Drayton isn't about to supply any."

Ana freshened his cup from the big coffeepot. "Fletch, what about the ore that has been dug out? Couldn't we raise more money on such col— My *inglés* is not good."

"Collateral? We'd hardly got out enough ore to provide it. I don't know what potential backers Alex meant to approach. He had all the connections, and his widow is not about to give us that information, either."

"Then Cordwainer has won?"

"For the time being."

Danny Mike lounged away from the wall. "Ah, it would be a damned pretty thing to see that old bastard over a gunsight sometime."

Ana's face held quiet shock. "You would do that, Danny? You would murder a man?"

"Murder? I'd call it justice. For Tom and all the others. Damn that old spalpeen to all Sheol!" Danny Mike spat the words out like pebbles. "We can't lay hands on his hired killer. And Jagger—"

"Is dead," Doc cut in coldly. "His crew will drift away now, and there's an end of it. What good would killing Cordwainer do?"

"He still wants our silver, don't he? He can always raise another gang of hardcases, can't he?"

"Maybe he's had enough. It's been costly for him, too. We'll wait and see."

"Wait, Christ!" Danny Mike flung open the door and went out, slamming it behind him.

Ana's troubled gaze met Doc's. "He acts sometimes like he is crazy. It has not gotten better, Fletch."

"I know." Resting an elbow on the table, Doc massaged

his eyelids with his thumb and forefinger. Then he dropped
his hand. "Forgot about Bernardo. How has he been?"

"Resting well. Biddie is sitting up with him."

Ana picked up the lamp and led the way to the back
room. Bernardo was snoring lightly on the cot, one big
crooked hand resting on his chest. His color was good, and
he had no fever.

Doc shook his head, grinning a little. The man's stamina
was fantastic. Only the first of the two bullets fired at
Bernardo had found its mark, and after the second missed,
he had simply played possum, lying immobile in the blazing
sun while his life bled slowly away. Yet after Doc had tied
off his wound, he'd easily held his saddle clear back to the
O'Hearn place. He'd taken a long draught of whiskey but
hadn't let out even a grunt as Doc probed for and extracted
the bullet and bandaged him up. Afterward he had protested
that he didn't need to go to bed. They had insisted, and now
Bernardo was sleeping like a baby. Like a baby bull,
thought Doc.

Biddie had fallen sound asleep, curled up in a big
rawhide-rigged armchair in the corner. Ana got a blanket
and spread it over her, and the girl never stirred. "We're all
tired," whispered Ana.

When she and Doc returned to the kitchen, she set the
lamp on the table and turned its flame low. Then she
straightened, her eyes meeting his.

"Well," he said awkwardly, "I had better turn in."

But he didn't move. He stood watching her in the dim
light. The moments ribboned on between them. Finally, she
said, "Now you will be going, Fletch? Away from us?

"I'm one of you, Ana. I thought by now you'd—" He
checked himself, only adding quietly, "Why would I go?"

Ana turned her face half away, lamplight glowing bronze
along the planes of her profile. "Because she is going. I
think she will want you to follow, no?"

Doc said tiredly, "No. She loved him very much, Ana."

"*A mi qué?* It did not make her stop caring for you. Long ago, you were first in her thoughts, it may be. But something happened. . . ."

Doc scowled. "Are you a witch or what, Ana?"

"I am a *peón* woman, Fletch. All *peónes* live close to the earth. Some of us, maybe, it turns into witches." Her tone was half playful, but her look wasn't. It questioned him fiercely.

"Whatever was or wasn't with me and Caro Drayton," he said slowly, "is done with. For me it is."

One of them must have moved first. But he never knew which it was, then or later. Only that she was in his arms, all of her fine lean body straining to him, all the curves and hollows molding as one to his flesh, the hunger of their mouths long and deep, and he did not know how long it lasted.

Finally, they broke apart a little, enough for Ana to say with a husky, soft-wild laugh, "Your gun—"

Doc realized its hard bulk had been pressed almost painfully between them. He pulled the Navy Colt from its shoulder holster and laid it on the table; then stared down at it for a long raw moment of realization. His fevered brain cooled, and he just looked at her.

"Fletch? What is it?"

Doc pulled gently away and walked a slow circle of the room, rubbing his right fist into his left palm. Her eyes followed him, somber and wondering. Finally, he hauled up in front of her.

"Your husband, Ana—"

"Yes?"

"I killed him."

"*Qué?*"

"I killed Tom O'Hearn. He was shot twice. My bullet killed him."

Now it was out, spoken at last. No matter what came of it, he couldn't have left it unsaid, unseen but festering between them. Flatly and without expression he told her how it had happened. He did it unsparingly and with no sense of self-pity. Only the easing of a terrible and futile regret.

And it was finished. He waited. It had been a day for endings, he thought obscurely. Here was another, smoldering in Ana O'Hearn's face as it came alive with all the passion of her Latin and Indian heritage, the hot blood of pure hate.

She snatched up his Navy Colt from the table, thumbed it to cock, and held it almost against his body. Her eyes snapped with black lights. Doc didn't move, bracing for the bullet. Later she will think, but not now, not now. . . .

He was wrong.

A long shudder ran through Ana. Carefully, she let the gun off cock and held it out, and he took it. Then she spoke at last, almost inaudibly. "I came close to killing you, gringo. If you ever come under this roof again, I will kill you. Get out. I hope your dreams are bad."

CHAPTER TWENTY

NEXT MORNING DOC AND DANNY MIKE SET OUT FOR Rincon in the spring wagon. It was time to lay in a fresh store of supplies, and Ana had given Danny Mike a list of what was needed. Doc, preoccupied and not hankering to stay around the place this morning, accompanied him.

It was a bright, cool day. Danny Mike seemed to enjoy it, clucking to the horses and humming loudly. He looked boyishly clear-eyed and contented, his acrimonious mood of last night forgotten. Presently he said, "How come you didn't show at breakfast, Doc? Ana whipped up a mess of flannel cakes. Boy! Good Anglo grub for a change. I get tired of all her pepper-gut cooking. But she sure slings a tasty flannel cake."

"I reckon I was feeling off my feed," Doc said absently.

Ana had forbidden him the house, but she hadn't quite given him his walking papers. And she obviously hadn't told Danny Mike what Doc had told her. She had cooled off a little, but what did it mean?

Doc had spent another near-sleepless night. He'd done a lot of thinking, but his brain only tracked in circles. He had no answers. Only a deathly feeling in his bones that still another attempt at finding happiness had gone awry. He hadn't realized how inextricably Ana had become enmeshed in his conviction that he had finally found a place where he belonged, a place of home and hearthside. Now he had cut it clean. Or so it seemed. She might repent the words spoken in hurt and anger. But would she ever forget that he'd pulled the final trigger on her husband?

They rode off the last heights, past Cordwainer's abandoned roadblock, and left the peace of the high country for the muscular hurly-burly of Rincon. Danny Mike pulled the wagon up by Markeson's General Merchandise Store, and he and Doc went inside to get the order filled. Soon they were wrestling barrels and gunnysacks of grub out of the store and into the wagon bed.

The labor was welcome. It roused the sluggish workings of Doc's body and brain. All right, he was through on the Flats. No deceiving himself on that score. He had to force himself in a new direction. Or go back to stagnating in Taskerville, drinking too much, going slack and soft, tinkering with the dregs of an aimless existence.

He had no taste for that way of living anymore.

Caroline. She was leaving here; she would be gone soon. What had Ana said? "I think she will want you to follow." Maybe it was true. Even if he and Caroline had lost a tenuous common hold on the past, what of the future? It was open-ended. Who could see to the end of what was still to come?

Doc heaved a sack of flour into the wagon bed and paused, his gaze lifting to the small cabin on the ridge side above Rincon. He had promised he would call on her again. Why not make it now?

Danny Mike came out of the store, toting a bag of potatoes. He slung it in the wagon bed and said, "Reckon that does it."

"All right. You in the mood for a beer?"

"Anytime. You buying?"

"Sure." Doc dug out a coin and handed it to him. "But I'm not joining you. I have to pay a call on somebody. You wait at the Shortbough and wet a whistle for both of us."

"That somebody wouldn't be Mrs. Drayton, would it?"

"Maybe. Any comment?"

Danny Mike grinned. "Nope. Just that you don't waste a lot of time, Doc."

Doc turned from the wagon but had hardly started downstreet when he came to a dead stop.

Bowie Sansone.

There he was, coming down the boardwalk on his stumpy legs, a slight man with thinning sandy hair. He wore a baggy linen duster, and his whiskers burred in a tobacco-stained ruff around his almost-chinless jaw. Beyond his surprise at seeing the man, what caught Doc's eye at once was the dirty sling that cradled Sansone's right arm.

"Bowie!"

He said it just loud enough to catch the man's attention. Bowie halted and turned his mild blue eyes on Doc. Not in the least taken off guard, he said genially, "Well, now, Fletch Styles," as he stepped off the walk and held out his good hand. "I be pluperfect damned. What you doing this far north?"

"I might ask you the same." Doc smiled as he shook hands.

But there was no need to ask. A piece of missing puzzle had already jigsawed into place.

Bowie Sansone was a veteran of some of the border country's bloodiest cattle wars. His wasn't a name bruited about in ordinary trail-side gossip, and for good reason. Bowie had never run with a gang and only rarely with the kind of casual troubleshooters with whom Doc had once associated. He was always the outsider, a lone wolf who undertook the quiet, dirty jobs for which few of even the worst badmen had stomach. Bowie was the ideal man for such work: paunchy and aging, looking almost ineffectual, the sort of nondescript drifter to whom you wouldn't give a second glance.

Doc knew him only slightly. Like Elmo Jagger's, Bowie

Sansone's gun was for sale to the highest bidder. But Bowie was a solitary killer. Never facing a victim outright, he murdered from hiding, from ambush. Always from concealment, always with a quick, efficient unexpectedness, then fading from the scene like a ghost. Doc wasn't acquainted with many such assassins, but enough that he hadn't been able to cinch the regulator's identity with any certainty.

Now he knew. Bowie Sansone wasn't this far off his usual stamping ground by chance.

Still wearing a pleased smile, Doc said, "What brings you to these parts, old booger?"

"Business. You?"

"Business."

Bowie showed a great yellow-toothed yawn of a grin. "Seems we both been tendin' to business, then. How's yours coming 'long, boy?"

"A mite better than yours, from the look." Doc nodded at Bowie's injured arm. "Caught some lead, did you?"

"Just a scratch. Had me stiffed up for quite a spell. She's coming along fine, though."

"Good."

"Ought to have this sling off 'er in another two, three days."

"Better yet."

They grinned into each other's faces like Cheshire cats and never batted an eye. It was an old game for both of them, and Doc felt a thin, vicious pleasure in playing it out in kind. Abruptly he reached out and jerked back the skirt of Bowie's duster. Sewed to its inner lining was a leather scabbard containing a sawed-off shotgun. Its weight had sagged the duster on that side.

"Still packing the old cutter, I see."

"Same old one," Bowie agreed, pulling the duster gently from Doc's hold and taking a step back. "Best thing for

close work. Even if a man pulls a mite slow, he can't hardly
miss."

"You always did fancy tall odds," Doc said, grinning.
"So long as they favored you."

"Yes, sir. I always did."

"But you never minded taking a long chance now and
then."

"Never did, nope. Keeps a man on his toes."

"Still, you're not used to coming off on any short end.
That arm must hurt like hell," Doc said.

"Like I said, it's almost healed up. Leaves a man
pluperfect pissed off, though."

"I'll bet it does. You fetch the son of a bitch who did it?"

"Nope. He is *numero uno* on my bait-a-coyote list."
Bowie tugged at his hat brim. "Got to be wobbling along,
boy. Be seeing you for sure. You—"

"Say, what is this?" Danny Mike burst out. "Who the
hell is this guy?"

Unnoticed by Doc, he had sidled up almost beside him.
He was scowling blackly and with a dawning realization.
Christ, he heard it all, thought Doc, and threw an arm
across Danny Mike's chest as he started forward.

"Just simmer down—"

Danny Mike batted the arm aside and moved past Doc.
His eyes wore a bright mad sheen as he stared at Bowie
Sansone. "You're the one," he whispered. "Jesus Christ!
You're the man!"

Bowie's eyes were as impersonal as a snake's. "Who is
this kid? Friend of yours?"

Doc caught Danny Mike by the shoulder, saying in a steel
voice, "Don't be a damned—"

Not turning, Danny Mike swept out a thick arm,
knocking Doc backward for a couple of staggering steps.
The same arm swung forward, all the weight of Danny
Mike's strong, stocky body behind it as the fist met Bowie's

face with a meaty crunch. Bowie was slammed over backward in the dust.

The regulator clawed back the duster skirt, his hand diving inside. Danny Mike's gun was already out and coming up. But Doc moved faster than either of them, his Navy Colt in hand as he took a long step. His arm chopped up and down, the Colt's muzzle rapping the kid's skull above the right ear. Without a sound, Danny Mike pitched forward on his face.

Doc said thinly, "You ease off that, Bowie," and waited till Sansone's fingers came out empty from under his slicker before leathering the Colt.

Bowie climbed to his feet, cupping a hand over his broken nose. Blood ribboned in two streams down the creases that bracketed his broad mouth. He dug out a bandanna and held it to his nose, saying mildly, "Kid's got a wild hair up his ass. It could just tickle a man to death. Who is he?"

"Danny Mike O'Hearn. Somebody deadfalled his brother a while back."

"Do tell." A fleeting amusement colored Bowie's faded eyes. "Got thinking it was me, eh?"

"Give Cordwainer a message from me, will you, Bowie?"

"Cordwainer?"

"Tell him he's won. The mine's closed off, and we're dead broke. Out of money. Just that. Tell him. And tell him there's no need for him to keep you on any longer. The fight is over."

After a moment Bowie bent over and picked his hat out of the dust. He beat it against his pants and set it on his head. He glanced at a handful of curious bystanders, then looked squarely at Doc.

"Who says it is?"

* * *

Doc didn't pay his call on Caroline Drayton. He loaded Danny Mike in the wagon bed with the supplies, then went back into the store and bought enough rations to last him a couple of weeks, paying for them out of his own pocket. Then he climbed up to the wagon seat and hoorawed the team into motion.

They were a mile out of Rincon when Danny Mike came to, groaning loudly. Doc didn't even glance around. He knew that the practiced tap of his gun barrel would leave the kid with a bad headache and nothing more except for a disinclination to raise a ruckus for a while.

"Come on up here," Doc said.

Danny Mike clambered laboriously over the seat back and dropped onto the seat beside Doc, giving him a groggy, furious look. "Where's my gun?"

Doc lifted the .44 from his belt and passed it to him.

"Goddam you, Doc. I had him dead. I had the bastard dead to rights. And you——"

Doc cut in. "Boy, even in Rincon there's vigilante law, if no other kind. A dozen people must have seen you knock him down. Then you pulled iron on him while he was flat in the dust. You'd have shot him dead, too."

"Damn right I would!"

"And in less than an hour a miner's jury would have you stretching hemp. These kangaroo courts don't waste time."

Danny Mike held a sullen silence clear back to the O'Hearn place, and then he set about unloading the wagon with a fury. Doc took his purchases to the cabin he shared with Bernardo and the kid. He'd prepare his own meals there and eat apart.

And he would wait. He wasn't moving on just yet. Bowie Sansone's last words to him had made it clear that in or out of Cordwainer's service, Bowie wasn't finished here. Doc had inflicted a humiliating defeat on him; Danny Mike had deepened the humiliation by breaking his nose—more than

enough to set a killer's pride on edge till his warped honor
was satisfied.

That meant drawing blood. Taking life. Maybe a hundred
other facets of revenge that Doc couldn't foresee. He
couldn't ride out on the O'Hearns now and leave them
saddled with that peril. Once more Danny Mike had been
lucky and didn't know it. All things equal, he'd stand less
than no chance against a seasoned killer like Sansone.

In the week that followed, Doc and Ana kept a cool
distance from each other, taking care that their separate
tasks on the place never brought them into proximity. Doc's
easy camaraderie with Bernardo continued, however. The
giant was on his feet in a few days, but at Doc's insistence
he confined himself to a few light chores. Predictably,
Danny Mike, in another of his disconcertingly sudden
switches, resumed his friendship with Doc as if nothing had
disturbed it.

One job that remained to be done on the roughly finished
buildings was the particularly slow and tedious one of
covering the roof planks with split-wood shingles. Doc and
Danny Mike sawed a number of seasoned logs into short
chunks. Then they enlisted the skills of Juan Caldeira and
his sons, who showed up one morning with the necessary
tools. While the Caldeiras tackled the intricate work of
splitting log chunks into shingles with vises and foot levers
and froes, Doc and Danny Mike carried baskets filled with
shakes up onto the house roof and nailed them into place.
Bernardo went about his usual chores.

At midday, Ana called the men in for the noon meal. Doc
washed up with the others, but as they filed into the house,
he headed for the bunk cabin. Seated on the doorstep, he
opened a can of tomatoes with his knife, speared out the
pulpy hunks, and drank off the cool juice. He ate a couple of
cold biscuits from a several-days-old scorched batch and

washed them down with black bitter coffee of his own brewing.

Old Juan came out of the house, munching a sandwich. He crossed the yard and sat down beside Doc with a grunt. "Jesus, *muchacho*. Wha's that you're eating? And that stuff, you call that coffee?"

"I never call it anything in polite company. Not that you qualify."

Juan Caldeira chuckled. "You an' her, you on the outs again, eh? She's say you are not welcome under the roof."

"She's conveyed that impression."

"Jesus, what's it this time? Always it's something. Maybe you better marry that woman, Juanito. Then you stay in the house and fight, but you eat good. Her and Tomás, Jesus, they had some beautiful fights. Sure, Juanito, you be ahead to marry her. Her taste runs to gringos."

"Not this one, *viejo*."

Old Juan picked his teeth contemplatively. "That is a pile of horseshit. When she says your name, it is like she is biting nails. From her this is a lot of feeling. I tell you— *uh*!"

An explosive grunt left Juan Caldeira. He buckled forward, his seamed face twisted with pain. The hammer clap of a shot drowned the midday silence in a shower of echoes. Seizing hold of Juan before he fell, Doc felt a warm torrent of blood pour over his hand. His gaze slashed across the wide stretch of trampled ground between the buildings. By a corner of the barn a pall of powder smoke was fraying away like grimy mist. Bowie Sansone stood there in plain sight, aiming his rifle again.

Shards of wood flew from the step inches from Doc's knee. Again the billow of smoke and gun roar. Then Sansone stepped back from sight and was gone.

Doc eased Juan down on his back and lunged to his feet, pulling his Navy Colt as he headed for the barn at a crouching run. He came hard against its north wall and edged along it till he reached the corner where Bowie had been. He looked cautiously past it.

Beyond the ranch's headquarters on that side, a mixture of pine and cedar grew heavily away toward the foothills. It was one of the few places on the Flats where the regulator might steal close to a settler's buildings, take a shot at someone, and then fade back out of sight. Elsewhere the humpy thin-grassed terrain would have provided little cover for his disappearing act. So his attacks had been confined to forested areas.

Doc swore bitterly. He simply hadn't considered that Bowie, for all his calm gall, would walk boldly onto the O'Hearn place and notch up a victim. It was too unexpected. And once again the regulator was gone, swiftly and silently as always.

Doc tramped back to the cabin. The shots had brought everyone from in the house on the run. At Doc's direction, two of Juan's sons carried him into the cabin and laid him on his back on the table.

Carlos, the oldest son, asked, "Is it bad?"

"Yes," Doc answered even before he opened Juan Caldeira's shirt and began his examination. The bullet had angled through his chest, narrowly missing the heart, and had emerged high on his right side. Doc had feared from the sudden rush of blood that an artery had been hit, but the flow from both holes was steady—no pumping of bright arterial blood. Unasked, Ana brought a kettle of hot water and strips of clean cloth for bandaging. As he worked on Juan, Doc's mind ran coldly over what had happened.

From that distance Bowie could have shot him as easily as Juan. He had placed his second shot extremely close, but not close enough to kill or even wound. It meant only one thing: this wasn't another cold piece of assassin's business to Sansone. He had issued a personal challenge.

Quietly, as he treated Juan's wound, Doc explained this to the others.

"We will go after him!" Angel, Caldeira's youngest son, declared hotly.

"No. I'll go alone. It's between him and me. If you trail along, he'll fade out of sight. He'll never show himself," Doc said.

Danny Mike leaned forward, his eyes intent and glassy bright. "Yeah. His fight is with you. Me, too. He's got it in for me just as much. I'm going with you. You can't stop me, by God!"

Doc tied off the wound and rocked back on his heels, giving Danny Mike a quiet, merciless scrutiny. "Why, boy," he said dryly, "I wouldn't even try."

CHAPTER TWENTY-ONE

In retreating this time, Bowie Sansone had made no effort to hide his trail. He wanted Doc to pick it up easily and follow it along the line of Bowie's own choosing. Doc knew instinctively that the regulator would head for terrain that no horse could negotiate. That was Bowie's way. A horse would only make an easy target. It would be like him to shoot a pursuer's horse just to drag the chase out a little further.

Juan Caldeira had been lucky. He'd been spared a mortal wound by an inch or so. Doc had no doubt that Bowie had shot to kill. Murdering one of Doc's friends would be the one sure way to bring Doc out on the hunt for him, no matter what the odds. Doc felt no assurance in reading Bowie's intentions so clearly. The regulator would expect as much of him. He'd want Doc to be aware of where all the odds lay: with the man who led the chase, who could order it along any course he devised.

Doc and Danny Mike were armed with a pistol and rifle apiece. They had plenty of ammunition. Each carried a rucksack of food, a canteen of water, a mackinaw coat, a blanket, and ground tarp. Doc had his high-powered field glasses. They'd had to balance between packing light and a possibility of running out of grub. They had enough to last a week, but Doc didn't expect the pursuit would continue nearly that long.

Bowie would force the issue. He would make it a contest of nerves, and he would press Doc and Danny Mike tightly. As if they, not he, were the pursued.

They followed Bowie's tracks through swaths of timber and over sparse-grassed flats, climbing into the foothills of the Sweetwaters, tending south and east but always climbing. The range was open and thinly wooded on the lower slopes, alternating between ragged belts of meadow and timber. They kept a careful lookout but saw nothing. Much of the time Bowie might have them spotted from a vantage ahead. His trail was fresh and clung to ground that took sign easily and held it for a long while. Doc was a better-than-fair country tracker, and he set as fast a pace as he dared. Neither he nor Danny Mike was accustomed to tackling long distances on foot. Doc spelled them with frequent rest stops, timing them with his watch.

They trekked through the long afternoon, during which all they saw was the regulator's steady trail. Doc had expected that it would be this way at first. Bowie would choose the time and place.

Doc called a halt well before daylight had faded enough to make tracking impossible. When a man was tired and hungry and irritable enough to feel his senses growing dull, it was time to quit for the day. They were high in the foothills now, the timber looming darkly around them, and it wasn't easy to locate a campsite open enough for Doc's taste. He found one at last in a rough circle of rock slabs that would shelter a fire from the bitter night wind starting to cut down off the high peaks.

They built no fire. There'd be no giveaway smoke or, as darkness closed in, patch of firelight to betray their position. Not, Doc thought bleakly, that it was likely to make much difference. Bowie, wherever he was, doubtless had their

position fixed right now. At least he couldn't work close to
this camp by using the terrain for cover.

Danny Mike, less than half Doc's age, wasn't as tuckered
out as his companion despite the slight limp he displayed.
After wolfing down his cold rations, he paced up and down,
one hand plunged in a deep pocket of his mackinaw coat,
the other gripping his rifle. He muttered incoherently to
himself.

"We'll each stand a watch," said Doc, rolling out his
ground sheet. "Since you're feeling so bright-eyed and
bushy-tailed, you can take the first one."

Danny Mike didn't reply. He ceased his muttering but
never glanced at Doc; just kept up a silent pacing. The last
gold glint of daylight varnished his eyes to blank saffron
slits. I wonder, thought Doc, just how close to going clean
off his head he is. . . .

At dawn they roused to cold sunlight. Now, since they'd
be moving on, Doc did build a fire and cook a meal. They
would need the hot food for warmth and strength against the
hours ahead. He also kept a watch on all horizons for smoke
in case Sansone had the same idea. Doc didn't expect to
spot anything, but there it was—a thread of gray lifting
above a rocky shoulder of the upper heights.

Danny Mike saw it only a few moments later; he went
frantic with eagerness. "There he is! Dammit, there he is!
Let's get moving!"

"First we break camp," Doc said. "Then we move. And
we don't rush it."

"Why not, for hell's sake?"

"He's amusing himself at our expense or just luring us
into a bushwhack. Either way, it's a long way to climb, and
there's no use wearing ourselves out."

It was midmorning when they made their wary approach
to Bowie's camp in a stand of scrub cedar. The fire had been
set to smoke for a long time, and of course the camp's
occupant was long gone. Danny Mike, in a frenzy, cursed

when he saw the arrow carved in the bark of a tree, directing them straight upward.

Doc felt a wry, tired amusement. Almost as much at Danny Mike's loony frustration as at Bowie's joke. He sobered the feeling, though, knowing that was how a man felt when he was starting to get utterly fed up—with cold, with climbing, with his own gnawing impatience, with this whole lunatic game. It was no state of mind in which to confront an enemy.

It was warm, and they were sweating profusely, though the sky had turned drab and overcast. That was bad. Not because rain would wipe out the trail—Bowie could devise other ways to keep them on his heels—but because dismal weather would make this business all the harder. Rain canceled visibility; thunder covered sounds.

They toiled onward and upward, picking up just enough sign to follow. Bowie seemed to have no particular goal; he meandered on soft ground that skirted outcrops and rocky stretches where he might easily have lost himself. It was a grueling and monotonous climb over terrain that was unchanging except to grow steeper and flintier.

They nooned at the base of a vast sprawling ridge that formed a midway fold of one soaring peak. The ridge was laced with deep gullies and covered with a litter of boulders from which patches of small gnarled pine poked. Doc gave the ridge a thorough look-over as they ate. It would make a splendid maze in which a killer might play cat and mouse with his victims.

Was that what Bowie Sansone had in mind? Had he led them to this place on purpose? Given Bowie's bushwhacking skills, which Doc couldn't remotely touch, he could have a lot of fun with them here.

The sky had a texture like gray porridge; clouds roiled across it, white thunderheads building above the peaks. A trace of wind had died off, and an uneasy silence hung all around, making Doc's skin crawl.

Danny Mike felt it, too. He kept staring at the ridge. Gobbling the last of his food, he said, "Let's get up there!"

"Slow," said Doc. "Slow now."

They crept like inchworms up a stark face of rock that lay dangerously open to a patch of timber a hundred yards above. Doc's nerves were on knife edge.

A shot came, whining off a boulder to their near right.

Doc saw a blur of powder smoke near the timber. Danny Mike screamed, "There he is! There he is!" and scrambled onward, pumping shots wildly.

Doc, about to dive for cover, changed his mind and dived for Danny Mike's legs instead, bringing him down. The boy screamed again, twisting a look backward over his shoulder, and seeing his face, Doc felt a raw shock. It was contorted in madness, eyes staring, spittle streaking his chin.

Danny Mike kicked savagely, his heel tearing a furrow along Doc's jaw, and kicked again, freeing himself, surging up to his feet. Doc let himself roll loosely backward, tumbling into a shallow ravine that split the escarpment.

An instant later the second shot came.

Danny Mike was flung brokenly across the rocks, crumbs of shale rattling away from his fall, dribbling down onto Doc, where he lay barely hidden.

Doc raised up just enough to see the sprawled body, head turned sideways, face inches from his. The boy's eyes were frozen in a last vivid stare. His lower jaw was torn nearly away, the teeth splintered to white shards in a crimson horror of flesh.

This is what I saved his life for, thought Doc. To bring him to this. What's the sense to it? Even if the kid had been ailing, worsening, from an unseen pressure on his brain . . . what was the sense?

"Bowie!"

His hoarse call brought only echoes in reply. Sansone had already given his answer—a bullet squarely in Danny

Mike's face. He had wiped out a minor annoyance as a man might brush aside an insect.

I'm the whole game now. How will he play me out?

Doc was effectively trapped where he lay, just out of Bowie's line of fire. If he made a break in any direction, he'd be seen. Bowie could easily gun him down anytime he wished. It would depend on how long and far the assassin meant to crowd his "game."

Nature took an effective hand as the first fat blobs of rain pelted down. Maybe the rain would be his ally, after all. Doc waited. In seconds the sky split open like a ruptured melon, torrents of water lashing the ridge side, fuming in curtains of mist off the bare rock.

Doc took his chance, leaping up and cutting sideways across the rugged slope, running, stumbling, sliding. He made for a deep fissure that slashed vertically back into the ridge. Bowie's rifle spoke from above, three quick shots, as if the assassin feared that some of his advantage had shrunk.

Doc felt a bullet burn along his calf. He dived inside the fissure and was again cut off from gunfire. He peered into the murky depths of the passage. It was really a small canyon, open at the top. Miniature waterfalls cascaded down the walls, and he could make out nothing in the thick spewing mist. At its mouth the split was hardly four feet wide, its narrow bottom angling upward as it penetrated the ridge. Maybe it would lead right up to Bowie's level—where Bowie would be waiting.

It was a chance he had to take.

Doc climbed steadily, clumsily, blindly up the slick-rocked floor of the fissure, unable to make out anything that lay ahead of him. Maybe his specs would help. He dug out his glasses and hooked them on, and then he could pick out near details, glistening abutments to his right and left, but not much else. He struggled on, realizing with a sinking sensation that the fissure was narrowing down and there was no open end in sight.

It pinched off suddenly. Bowie had maneuvered him into a cul-de-sac.

Doc crouched down, soaked and shivering, watching behind him and above him. Bowie could shoot downward from the rim or work inside the fissure for a shoot-out. Or he could wait outside. The first way would be too easy, like potting a sitting duck. By now he might be close to the fissure entrance, or inside it, hidden by the crabbed bends of the passage. The cramping walls around Doc tapped deadly wellsprings of panic deep within him. Cornered like a rat.

He could turn back and face Bowie in the passage or outside it. Either way, the assassin would have the advantage.

Doc peered up, blinking at the murky wedge of sky overhead. Was there a chance he could muscle himself upward along the fissure's end where the walls veed together? A damned slim chance. There were no handholds this far down, but maybe there was a way. Bowie might never suspect he'd try it, and that knowledge decided Doc.

He had rigged a sling on his rifle, and now he hooked it over one shoulder. Bending at the knees and bracing himself, he sprang upward, ramming his doubled fist into the V-shaped crack. The pain as his dangling weight wrenched against the hold was excruciating. Doggedly he clenched the other fist and inserted it above the first, relaxing that to take a higher hold, dragging himself upward by agonizing inches.

After two torturous feet of ascent, Doc's brain was a red fog of anguish. Then the crack started to widen and presented, just within reach, a knob of rock he could grip with one bleeding hand. Putting out all his strength, he hauled his whole body upward till it fit into the slowly widening crevice. Finally, he could brace his back against one side of the rock chimney, his bent knees against the other.

Above the hissing rattle of rain, he thought he heard a scrape of sound, maybe a boot sole on rock, somewhere in the passage. If Bowie was coming—if he caught his prey like this . . .

With a furious burst of energy Doc used his knees, elbows, hands, to fight upward. His toes gained purchase on the wet rock now, and the rim was only inches away. He reached up far enough to grip it with one hand, twisted to take a grip with the other hand, too, then jackknifed his body up and over the lip rock, flopping there like a grounded fish.

Bowie fired from below, the bullet screaming off rimrock as Doc rolled back away from it.

He lay sprawled and exhausted, straining his ears. No other sound from down there. He sat up, examining his savagely torn hands. The skin across his knuckles was in bloody shreds, and he could barely move the fingers. Could he hold a rifle? He unslung the weapon, wrapped his hands around it, and forced his fingers into motion. Then he got to his feet, swaying dizzily. The rainy scape blurred around him.

Now, at least, he was above Bowie Sansone. It was a psychological edge, not a physical one: accurate shooting on a downhill angle was a sight harder than drawing a bead uphill.

Bowie wouldn't even consider ascending the fissure's end where Doc, waiting above, could nail him on the climb. The regulator would fade back toward the entrance. Now, if Doc moved quickly, Bowie might be the trapped one.

Doc clambered back along the rim as fast as he could, not looking into the mist-clogged fissure where, even now, Bowie would be stumbling along parallel to him, hampered by the worsening pound of rain.

Doc's feet skidded; he took a jolting fall. His glasses flew off and broke, shards of both lenses tinkling among the rocks. Damn! He scrambled up and onward and came to a stop above the fissure mouth just as Bowie emerged from it.

Doc threw his rifle to his shoulder and took a snap shot at

the man's dark form and missed. He took the time to steady
his aim, blinking nearsightedly as he tried to line the blurred
sights. He squeezed off the shot almost blindly and missed
again.

Bowie was wheeling into the open now, turning, pumping off shots. Doc felt the smash of a bullet in his left side,
another in his left arm—a shattering blow. The rifle spun
from his grasp.

Doc dropped to his knees, shaking his head, trying to
clear it against the impending oblivion, induced by crushing
pain. Bowie was hoofing it up the slope toward him now,
not hurrying.

"Styles—" His voice was hoarse with laughter. "Styles,
you ever see a man after he's been left to die with both his
elbows and both his knees busted by bullets? No . . . you
save 'em, don't you? Other way around with me. I've shot
'em and left 'em—"

Halting, he started to pull a careful bead on Doc's sound
arm. But that one was already in motion, with a speed that
no rifleman could match. Doc's hand plunged into his coat
and came out with the Navy Colt. In the instant it hung
level, he fired.

Bowie Sansone, looking for an easy kill, had walked into
pistol range. He rocked back with the bullet's impact. His
dark wet form seemed to pull together, dissolving into itself
as Doc fired again. Bowie's rifle went off, discharging
orange flame into the ground ahead of him. Then he was
falling forward.

Doc was falling, too, leaving the last shred of awareness
of a rain-gray world for utter darkness.

CHAPTER TWENTY-TWO

HE SLID IN AND OUT OF DARKNESS FOR A LONG TIME, A hazy drift of faces and voices and sensations. He was seldom alone—he knew that much—and there wasn't much pain. Always he sank back into a warm well of oblivion and was grateful for it.

The time came when he could open his crusted eyelids and be reasonably, if weakly, aware of his surroundings. He was in the familiar back room of the O'Hearn house, and Ana was there, too. It was night; a low-turned lamp glowed on a commode, and she was dozing in the big armchair.

He blinked a few times and, deciding this was reality, croaked out a few words, trying for speech. Ana awoke at once. Her face didn't tell him much, but she came quickly to his side.

"Fletch?"

"Indeed," he whispered. "I'll be hanged. I'm still alive."

"Of course you are. Thanks to Bernardo."

"Didn't mean that. Thought if I ever came under your roof again, you'd plumb salivate me."

She said something in reply, but he forced a wisp of smile to his lips and felt himself slipping the thread of reality again.

It was morning when he came fully awake. The morning

after that same night, he knew, for his sense of time had
returned. He was able to take a little warm broth; Ana
spooned it into his mouth while she told him how he'd
gotten here.

On the morning following the afternoon that he and
Danny Mike had gone after Bowie Sansone, Bernardo had
set out on their track, unmoved by warnings that he was in
no condition for it. He went on horseback, accompanied by
Juan Caldeira's stalwart sons and a remuda of spare horses.
By that evening a heavy storm had wiped out the trail, but a
little farther on they had found Danny Mike and Bowie and
Doc. Bernardo and the Caldeira boys had buried Bowie,
loaded the body of Danny Mike on a horse, and fashioned
an Indian-style travois to bring Doc home on.

Doc had raged with a deep fever for two days, during
which Dr. Kroll, summoned from his long sojourn in the
mountains, had treated the wounds. One bullet had gone
clean through his arm, breaking the elbow, and the other
had been dug out of his side by Kroll.

Doc looked at his hands resting on the coverlet. Both
were heavily bandaged. He could move the right one
without difficulty, but even stirring the fingers of the left one
sent a shock of pain nearly to the shoulder. That arm was
splinted and bandaged tightly. Moving his body brought
more pain.

"He did some digging, all right," Doc said morosely. "I
can feel it clear to my toes. The old butcher. I suppose he
was drunk? *Borracho?*"

"Only a little," said Ana. "Biddie and I have taken turns
watching you. And Mrs. Drayton has been here."

"Caro? She hasn't—"

"She has not left for the East, no." Her face was still and
solemn. "I sent one of the Caldeiras to tell her you were
hurt, and she has been here twice. Once each day."

"Uhm." Doc stared at the hand-hewn beams overhead,
wondering what the hell else to say.

"You should have more broth," said Ana. "I will bring you some."

She walked to the doorway and then paused to look at him, her face wooden and unreadable. "I would say this. I know you had to tell me about Tom. It was honest of you. But I don't want Biddie to know, ever. There is no need. It is enough that you and I know. Only us."

Doc opened his mouth to reply, but she'd already passed into the next room. When she returned with the broth, her manner was so stern and remote that he said nothing. She'd chosen a time when Biddie was absent from the house to say what she had to say, he supposed glumly. And that was that.

The beef broth was hot and strong and tasty, and he drank three cups of it.

The next day he ate a little solid food and traded acid witticisms with Dr. Kroll, who was making a long-neglected round of calls on his country patients. Kroll examined Doc and said he was sorry to see him getting better—it might lower the life expectancy of other citizens by quite a lot—but maybe this would serve him a lesson.

"What lesson?" asked Doc. "That bullets will get a man dead a sight faster than booze?"

Dr. Kroll snorted. "My dear colleague, if I didn't know that, I'd be dead these many years. No, I refer to your left arm. Did the best repair job I could on that smashed capitulum, but I'm afraid the arm will be stiff as a stick the rest of your days."

"I guessed as much."

"Too bad it wasn't your shooting arm, but the world wouldn't be that lucky."

After Kroll left, Doc gave the matter a good deal of sober thought. In all his reckless living since the war, he hadn't been touched by lead once. Now he had been tagged three times, counting the bullet that had nicked his calf. Doc was no believer in omens, but he believed profoundly in mortality. It was time to hang up the guns for good. If fate and Cordwainer would let him.

Maybe fate gave him a reply of sorts. Less than an hour after Kroll's departure, he had a second visitor. This one was brought into the room at gunpoint by Carlos Caldeira, who had spotted the man headed toward the O'Hearns' and had overtaken him.

He was a stocky white-haired man in rumpled but expensive riding clothes. With no inkling at all of what Matthew Cordwainer looked like, Doc knew at once that this was he.

"This man wants to see you," said Carlos. "He won' say who he is or what his business is."

"Does he have a gun?"

"He had the *pistola*. I took it."

"*Gracias*. Will you wait outside, then, Carlos?"

When Carlos had tramped out of the house, Doc said pleasantly, "Have a seat. Did you come here to give up?"

"No," Cordwainer said bluntly. "I've come to break the opposition for good and all."

"Uh-huh. I thought Jagger and Sansone were supposed to do that."

"They're dead. You're the man who walked over both of them, and you're alive. You're the opposition, Styles. The backbone of it, anyway. I want you out of the fight. If the only way I can get you out is to buy you out, I'll do it."

Fight for what? Doc wondered wryly. With no financial backing, the Flats people were already stopped cold. Aloud he said only, "And suppose you can't?"

"I don't just want you out of here, Styles. I want you on my side. My offer is half of whatever we'll make out of the Redondo silver range after you rid it of this hybrid trash you've been abetting."

Doc was silent for some moments, weighing the magnitude of what Cordwainer had just offered: an easy dirty fortune. Then he said mildly, "Trash is a relative term. Coming from you, it's sort of like finding a dewdrop in a nest of maggots."

Cordwainer nodded with no surprise or rancor. "A man can only try. I thought there might be an outside chance, at least, that we could make a deal."

"We can," said Doc. "You leave us alone, and we'll leave you alone. How's that?"

Cordwainer's only reply was a crooked smile, but Doc had a feeling this was the end of the trouble. At least from that direction.

On other counts he felt less than sure of anything. Ana was pleasant and attentive, and he must have regained a little ground there. But although he threw out several awkward ploys in an effort to determine what she really felt, she wouldn't give him an inkling. He also wondered why Caroline hadn't come visiting today. Not that he had a right to expect her to, and it was quite a long ride. But something still wasn't quite resolved between them.

Just how preoccupied Doc was showed in his checkers game that evening. Bernardo beat him three out of four games.

Shortly before noon of the following day, the giant was on his way to repeating that accomplishment when they heard a rider come into the yard, then the voices of Caroline and Ana in an exchange of polite greetings.

Their game was only half finished, but Bernardo dumped the checkers back in the box and folded up the board. He rose to his hulking height, gave Doc a solemn wink, and walked out of the room.

Caroline entered. She was wearing a trim riding habit, black for mourning, and a flat straw topper with a wisp of black veil. After the hellos were said, she took off the hat and her gloves, laid them on the bureau, and sat down in the chair Bernardo had vacated.

Doc caught the faint scent of her sachet, and her sudden smile completed a picture of dark beauty. Sometimes, he thought dourly, a woman was so damned stunning, so overwhelming to a man's senses, that it threw every honest feeling he had about her out of balance. Was that her fault or his?

For lack of anything better to say, he told her of Cordwainer's visit and his belief that the mining war was ended. She listened but then only nodded abstractedly.

"Fletch . . ." She reached out to touch his nearest arm, the left one. Remembering then, she drew her hand back. "I'm so glad to know you're better. I couldn't have left without being sure."

"You're still leaving, then?"

"On tomorrow's stage." She was silent a moment, head bent, kneading a pleat in her skirt. "I've done a great deal of thinking since— It was the shock of Alex's death, you know. . . ."

"Sure."

"But you only said the truth, and I didn't want to face it. Now—I want the Flats people to have what they were promised, what's rightfully theirs. I'll provide all the money they need to develop the mine."

Doc said quietly, "You're sure?"

"Very sure. Let it be an interest-free loan, payable when the profits are realized. Otherwise I want no part of the enterprise. It will be a memorial of sorts to Alex. To his ideals, his beliefs, his determination. I feel it would be only right. Don't you?"

"I think it's fine, Caro," he said slowly, "but I'm not the man to ask."

"Why not?"

"Maybe I want no part of it, either."

"Ah—" Her eyes widened; her voice caught softly. Then she bent quickly to him. Their lips met in a long warm kiss. When she drew back at last, her gaze was puzzled and searching.

"It's not the same any longer," she whispered, "is it?"

He said nothing. But he knew she was right. Something—something was still there. But it wasn't enough. Too much of it had burned out with time, with living. They were no longer the people they had been, and the pull of nostalgia wasn't enough. The last of his confusion had faded, and he wanted to tell her. But there was no need. Caroline's expression, sad and contained and gently smiling, held its own understanding.

She rose and walked quickly to the bureau. She pulled on her gloves and adjusted her hat and veil with jerky movements, as if in a hurry to be away now. Then she paused, saying abruptly, "Fletch, you'll be a part of it all. Like it or not, you *are*. You'll stay here, and you'll help them make Alex's dream a reality."

"What the hell, Caro," he said roughly. "I'm no mining man."

"But Alex had friends that are. Friends who had the deepest respect for his ability. More than one, I can assure you, will be eager to invest his talents in so promising a venture. . . ."

When she was gone, he lay for a while in the noonday calm, listening to the sounds of Ana and Biddie at work in the kitchen. They were talking a little, their voices so low-pitched that he figured he was the subject.

Doc gazed up at the ceiling beams and laid a bandaged hand on the log wall by his bunk. Solidity. Roots. A belonging.

"Ana," he called.

She came to the doorway and no farther, her dark eyes unquestioning, not quite aloof. She didn't speak.

"Ana, she is gone."

"I can see that. Gone for good?"

"Yes, damn it! For good."

"You wanted this?"

"Damn it, we both did. Now will you come over here. Can we talk to each other?"

"That is up to you."

"Up to me, is it? Come over here."

Ana laughed quietly and came to him.

MAX BRAND

THE BELLS OF SAN FILIPO

"Brand is a topnotcher!"   —*New York Times*

Year in and year out, Jim Gore wanders the barren hills of the Southwest, dreaming of mining the mother lode. Yet for all his schemes and hard work, the cunning saddle bum never figures on an earthquake uncovering a huge treasure in silver—and plunging him neck deep in dollars and danger. It seems that Gore isn't the only hombre who has a claim on the loot, and if he ever runs out of bullets, he won't be the only fortune hunter buried in the ghost town called San Filipo.

_3819-6 $3.99 US/$4.99 CAN